Graves-Hume

1401 West Main St.
Mendota, IL 61342
graveshume.org

D0560216

Hole in the Wall

Tevin Hansen

Handersen Publishing LLC
Lincoln, Nebraska

Handersen Publishing, LLC
Lincoln, Nebraska

Hole in the Wall

Text copyright © 2014 Tevin Hansen
Illustration copyright © 2014 Shaun Cochran
Cover copyright © 2015 Handersen Publishing, LLC
Cover Design Handersen Publishing, LLC

Summary: Evan Jacobson becomes trapped in his own imagination. He meets some strange new friends, finds himself in numerous adventures, and must complete three quests so he can get back home.

[1. Humorous stories—Juvenile Fiction. 2. Action and adventure—Fiction. 3. Magic—Juvenile Fiction. 4. Fantasy—Juvenile Fiction. Friendship—Juvenile Fiction.]

ISBN-13: 978-1-941429-54-9

Publisher Website: www.handersenpublishing.com
Publisher Email: editors@handersenpublishing.com
Author Website: www.tevinhansen.com

For Ellie and GoGo

INTERRUPTION:

The Storyteller Guy is sincerely sorry for this interruption—even though nothing has happened yet—but thought it should be stated that if you, the reader, come across any part of this story that seems too ridiculous to be true...

Just roll with it, people!!!

Sincerely,
The Storyteller Guy.

Chapter 1

The Broken Unicorn

Evan Jacobson is the most cynical kid you could ever meet. He is easily bored, very hard to please, and hates new ideas. Evan is definitely the most cynical kid at Lincoln Elementary School—except for Travis Spuzzum. Now *that* kid is cynical. And who wouldn't be with a name like Travis Spuzzum?

The point is this: Evan doesn't like <u>*anything*</u>. Nothing is good enough, cool enough, loud enough, quiet enough, big enough, small enough, near enough, far enough, crunchy enough, chocolaty enough, sweet enough, fun enough, exciting enough . . . (*okay, you get the picture.*)

It was Saturday. It was also time for Evan to get up and do his chores.

"Evan!" Mother called. "Wake up, sleepyhead! It's time to do your chorsies!"

Evan was wide awake now. Who can sleep with a yelling mom anyway? On top of that, he hated it when mother called them "chorsies." Something as awful as housework should not have a cutesy-wootsy name like chorsies. What Evan hated more than their name was actually *doing* them.

"EVAΛΛΛΛAN! Your father is waiting!!"

"Okay mom! Be right down!" Evan shouted, then pulled the covers up over his head and tried to go back to sleep.

Suddenly, through the bedroom window he heard Mr. Jacobson (*Evan's Dad, in case you weren't sure*) crank up the junky old lawnmower. The noise caused Evan to spring out of bed in a hurry. The number two rule of the Jacobson household was NEVER KEEP FATHER WAITING. The number one rule, of course, was NEVER KEEP MOTHER WAITING.

"On the double, buster!" Mother shouted. "I mean it!"

"I said I was coming! Geesh! Keep your pants on, lady!" Evan yelled back, of course keeping the last

5

comment to himself. Evan got dressed quickly, complaining quietly to himself about cruelty to children.

"EVAN JACOB JACOBSON! DOWNSTAIRS THIS INSTANT!" Mother yelled from the bottom of the steps.

Evan rushed past her and into the kitchen to check his to-do list. They were as follows:

—Mop the kitchen floor
—Sweep the porch (front <u>and</u> back)
—Dust the living room

All three of these chores sounded roughly the same, but he had to do them or else risk getting into trouble—or worse, getting sent to his room. Evan discovered ages ago that he couldn't stand being locked up in a room all by himself. He was far too cynical, and he ended up getting on his *own* nerves. And so, just because he felt like it, he did his list of chores in the reverse order.

This would prove to be a huge mistake.

"Okay, honey-pie!" Mother called a few minutes later. "I'm off to the grocery store!" This is what mother did every Saturday while the men did their share of the housework.

"Bye, Mom!"

At the exact same time she was getting ready to leave, Evan was busy dusting the inside of the glass display case in the living room. The very same glass display case where mother kept all of her antique crystal figurines, including her favorite one: a crystal unicorn that was handed down by her Great-Great Grandmother, then her Great-Grandmother, then her Grandmother, who accidently tried to sell it at a garage sale, but fortunately caught her mistake in time.

"See you in a few hours!" Mother called. "Be careful! And please don't break anything!"

C   R   A   S   H   !

Too late.

"What was that, Evan?" Mother asked, poking her head back inside the door.

"Nothing, Mother!" Evan lied. "Have fun exchanging green paper rectangles for food and stuff!"

"Okay then! See you in a few hours!"

If it was possible to sweat bullets, then that is *exactly* what Evan would be doing at this very moment. The crash wasn't *nothing*. It was *something*, all right. It was Great-Great-Grammy's antique unicorn figurine, the one that was just explained to you. All he'd been doing was simply waving the feather duster around wildly, paying absolutely no attention to what he was doing, trying to get the job done as quickly as possible. Just this *tiny* oversight resulted in the CRASH sound you just heard.

This was bad. This was very bad. This was *extremely* very bad. Evan needed to find a way to fix the broken unicorn, and quickly. If he couldn't fix it, then he'd probably be shipped off to some Scandinavian country— Denmark, for example—and forced to sing and dance for the rest of his life. All kinds of terrible thoughts started going round and round inside his cynical mind. Then suddenly, all of a sudden, the whole world seemed to be asking him if everything was hunky-dory.

Brrring! Brrring!

Grammy on the telephone: "Is everything all right, Evan? I had the most awful dream that something broke."

"Just fine, Grammy! No broken crystal unicorn figurine here!"

"Okay, sweetie! Just called to check. Say hi to your father for me!"

Two seconds later, father was sticking his head through the back door and asking if everything was all right. "Hm. That's strange? Thought I heard a crystal unicorn figurine crash on the floor?"

"No, Dad! Mom's crystal unicorn thing is right where it always is! Still in the glass display case and still in one piece!"

Evan snapped out of it. "Glue," he said. "Lots and lots of glue. I'll just glue it back together and no one will ever know the difference."

There was just one problem with this plan. Getting the glue meant going down into the basement. And going down into the basement meant *another* thing—

THE WASHING MACHINE MONSTER

Every kid knows that basements are full of monsters. So why do adults insist on putting important stuff like glue down there? Can't they *see* the monsters? Not *hear* them? Not *smell* them? Awful, terrible, scary things happen to children in basements. Some kids go into the basement and disappear forever. Some kids go into the basement and get so scared that their hair turns white. And *some* kids go into the basement and discover a hole in the wall which leads to a strange new world filled with all sorts of weird creatures.

"That's all baby stuff," Evan told himself while standing at the top of the stairs, hesitating, looking down into the creepy basement. "Eleven steps down, eleven steps back up. C'mon, Evan. You can do it."

1...2...3...4...5...6...

Evan stopped. There was a strange noise that caused his heart to start thumping loudly in his chest and put a big lump in his throat. Evan listened, then relaxed when he realized it was just the furnace kicking on.

"It's just the furnace, silly. Nothing to be scared of down here...especially not monsters."

7...8...9...10...11

Evan made it to the bottom of the steps without disappearing forever, which was good, or having his hair turn white, which was also good. Now all he had to do was take three big jumps over to the table with the glue on it, then take three big jumps back. That was all.

Evan could see the bottle of glue just a few feet away. It was on the table right next to the washing machine. Evan's three big jumps were typed in numerical order (*just like the steps*) so that everyone reading knew exactly what was going on.

1...2...3

"Yes!" Evan cried as he grabbed the bottle of glue from the table. "No ridiculous monster is going to get Evan Jacobson! No stupid monster will ever get—"

"*Grrrrrrrr!*" came a terrible growl behind him.

The Washing Machine Monster was alive!

"AHHHH!!" Evan screamed. Then he ran for his life. It was only three steps back to the staircase, but he tripped over his own feet during the second jump. The glue went flying. So did Evan. He felt a tremendous ka-thump on his forehead right before he face-planted the floor.

And...

...that's

...all

...he

...remembered.

Chapter 2
A Poem

Hole in the wall
Sh-mole in the wall
What do you mean there's a TROLL
In the wall?

I've been to a shopping mall,
And a bathroom stall,
Who cares about a stupid hole in the Wall?
Hole-y Swiss cheesecake!
There really IS a hole in the wall!?!

Do <u>not</u> go through the hole in the wall.

Chapter 3
Mr. Jenkinsen the Grouchy Troll

Evan escaped the Washing Machine Monster by mere inches. He knew that he'd never make it to the steps in time, so his only chance of escape was the big gaping hole between the freezer and the junk shelf. The very same hole that was *usually* covered by a steel grate, but which had conveniently fallen off, providing him with an escape route.

A hole in the wall.

"A-ha!" Evan cried victoriously. "I'll just slip into that hole in the wall. Nothing bad or strange can happen to me in *there*!!"

Soon Evan was crawling through the dirty, smelly, disgusting tunnel on his belly. His clothes were getting filthy, which would not make Mother happy. Evan

15

assumed she would rather have him dirty than gobbled up for lunch by a monster.

"Everything is hunky-dory," Evan told himself. "Father will come looking for me soon, so I'll just stay right here." Evan was safe for now. Safe and sound, hidden from all dangerous mechanical monsters that may or may not be a figment of his wild imagination.

"Father will come and rescue me any minute now…" Evan thought out loud, which is pretty much the same as saying it out loud. "Basement Monsters *never* attack adults. Every kid knows that. It's against the rules."

Evan waited in the dark, creepy, cramped tunnel for what felt like a very long time. Soon he began to doubt whether he was going to be rescued after all. He might have to rescue himself.

"What *is* this weird place, anyway?" he asked no one in particular. "And how come I never noticed it before?"

Evan had never noticed this tunnel before. He also thought it was kind of weird.

"I just said that!!" Evan shouted at the strange voice that came out of nowhere.

"*Huh? Oh, sorry,*" said the Storyteller Guy. "*Didn't mean to interrupt your conversation with yourself. Let's get back to the story, shall we?*"

"Okay, fine," Evan said as he rolled his eyes. "Hurry up, will ya? This place is kind of—"

"*Dark and spooky?*" suggested the Storyteller Guy.

"You got it."

(Hole in the Wall continues on the next page.)

(continued)

After a little while longer of nothing happening, just to keep the story moving along, Evan thought he heard some noises coming from the far end of the spooky tunnel. It was difficult to tell just exactly what the noise was, but if he had to make a *guess*...he would have guessed that it was a six-foot-tall troll rummaging through a cupboard.

"Hello?" Evan said. "Is anyone there?"

All of a sudden a grotesque green hand with long dirty fingernails came shooting out of the darkness. The scaly green fingers wrapped around Evan's ankle and began to drag him deeper into the tunnel.

"Hey, let go!" Evan yelled at the hand, but meaning to yell at whatever creature the hand belonged to. He kicked his foot with his other foot, if that makes any sense, and tried to crawl back through the tunnel and into the basement. This was no good either, since at the other end was the Washing Machine Monster waiting to chew him up and spit out the bones.

"What should I do?!" Evan asked, looking to the audience for help. "I'll be in danger no matter which way I

go! Isn't the suspense *killer*?!"

If it was a choice between a Washing Machine Monster that may or may not be real and a creature with scaly, green, claw-hands with dirty fingernails…Evan thought he would much rather take his chances with the Washing Machine Monster.

Suddenly, with surprisingly sudden suddenness, Evan was pulled clear through the tunnel by the long green scaly arm. He cried out in pain after he emerged from the tunnel, where he fell several feet and landed on his bottom-side.

Evan was in somebody's kitchen. Not some scary cave with a huge pile of kid skeletons like he'd imagined, but a regular old kitchen. There were cupboards, shelves, a pantry, a stove, and a refrigerator with pictures of baby trolls on it. It looked like a regular old boring kitchen…except for the hideous *troll* standing in it.

"AHHHH!" Evan screamed, but then stopped screaming when the hideous troll screamed at him to stop screaming, if that makes any sense.

"Oh, stop your screaming," said the troll, glaring at him with its arms crossed. "You're giving me a headache. Besides, you landed on your nice cushy bottom, so no harm done."

Evan's previous guess was very close, but not entirely accurate. It was not a six-foot-tall troll rummaging through a cupboard that he'd heard after all. It was a *seven*-foot-tall troll that he'd heard rummaging through a cupboard. And this troll did *not* look happy. This troll looked disgruntled, and mean, and cranky, and cantankerous, and every other word you can think of that means exactly the same thing.

Evan stood up and stared the troll down, while having to look *up* to meet his eyes.

"Who are you?" the troll demanded. "What are you doing in my cupboard? You're one of the king's spies, aren't you? Well, you just tell that chubby little fellow that I have paid my taxes—*in full.*"

Evan had no idea what the troll was talking about. He

knew nothing about kings, or spies, or taxes.

"Who am *I*?" Evan said, trying not to show any fear. "Who are *you*?!" Normally, if he saw a real live troll he would've been scared out of his mind. However, it was hard to be scared of a troll that looked exactly like his grouchy neighbor, Mr. Jenkins. Of course, Mr. Jenkins didn't have green skin, yellow eyes, and a mouth full of pointy teeth. Other than these few *minor* differences, this ugly creature looked pretty much the same as Mr. Jenkins, the meanest neighbor on the whole block, who kept every ball that ever landed in his front yard.

"I'm Mr. Jenkinsen," said the troll who looked just like Mr. Jenkins. "And you are *not* a rice cake. I was digging through the cupboard and looking for those awful rice cakes that Mrs. Jenkinsen makes me eat. Instead of a disgusting tasteless rice cake, I found a disgusting, tasteless child. Who are you? Where did you come from? And what were you doing in my cupboard?"

"My name is Evan Jacobson," Evan told the troll. "And what do you mean where did *I* come from? I came from that tunnel you just pulled me out of!"

Mr. Jenkinsen regarded Evan for a moment, then he

scratched his large scaly head. He looked up at his cupboard and then back down at Evan.

"What tunnel?" Mr. Jenkinsen asked. "You weren't in any *tunnel*, you twerp. You were in my cupboard! You were trying to steal my rice cakes! Thief! THIEF!"

"I am not a thief!" Evan said. "I'll show you what tunnel I'm talking about." Then he climbed up onto the countertop. "The tunnel that's right—"

There was no tunnel.

There was only a cupboard filled with high-fiber cereal, spices, and a half-eaten bag of rice cakes pushed off to one side. The half-eaten bag of rice cakes fell onto the countertop at Evan's feet.

"THIEF!" Mr. Jenkinsen hollered. "Rice cake stealer in my kitchen! Police! Swat Team! HELP!!!"

"I am *not* trying to steal your stupid rice cakes!" Evan told him as he jumped down off the counter. He handed the package of low-calorie, low-fat rice cakes to the troll. "Here."

"But? But? Are you *sure* you don't want to steal them?" Mr. Jenkinsen waved the rice cakes in Evan's face. "I really wouldn't mind letting you steal them? They taste awful!

Go on, take them. I'll just tell Mrs. Jenkinsen that I ate them all. She'll be so happy with me that she'll make me a nice juicy steak dinner with garlic toast and a baked potato covered in butter and sour cream." Mr. Jenkinsen licked his scaly lips and rubbed his huge belly just thinking about it.

"Listen up, Mr. Troll-person, or whatever your name is—" Evan folded his arms and tried to act tough, even though he barely came up to the troll's huge thunder thighs. "I don't want your stupid rice cakes, okay? My mother makes my father eat those nasty things because she says he's getting a big fat jiggle-belly. Just like yours."

Mr. Jenkinsen looked ashamed. He reached down and wiggled his jiggly stomach.

"I want to go home," Evan demanded. "*Now*, if you don't mind."

"I DO NOT HAVE A BIG FAT JIGGLE BELLY!" Mr. Jenkinsen roared, suddenly becoming very upset and speaking in capital letters. "I GREW TOO FAST WHEN I WAS YOUNG! AND I CAN'T EXERCISE BECAUSE I, UM...BECAUSE I HAVE ALLERGIES! SO THERE!"

Evan refused to believe him. This only infuriated the dieting troll even more.

"Listen up, you little brat," Mr. Jenkinsen said, his green face turning red with anger. "If Mrs. Jenkinsen hadn't put me on a diet, I would eat you right now, dipped in barbeque sauce, otherwise you would taste disgusting. But since she'll be home from the grocery store any minute, she would probably catch me green-handed. Then she'll make me stay on this terrible diet even longer! And since your tunnel—the one you *claim* exists—doesn't exist any longer, I'm afraid it's time for you to leave. *Now*, if you don't mind."

"But I have nowhere to go!" Evan protested. "I was just in my basement. Now I'm in *your* weird world and I can't get back."

"Not my problem," Mr. Jenkinsen said, shooing Evan out of the kitchen with a broom. "Out! Out! OUT!"

Evan was pushed right out the front door.

"And don't come back!" Mr. Jenkinsen shouted before slamming the door shut. Then he stuck his fat head out of the side window and yelled, "If you kick a ball into my yard . . . I'M KEEPING IT!"

Evan stuck his tongue out at the grumpy troll. Mr. Jenkinsen returned the gesture, only *his* tongue was purple, two feet long, and pronged like a fork.

"Just terrific," Evan said, brushing himself off. "I'm all dirty, I haven't finished my chores, and a troll just kicked me out of his house for stealing his rice cakes. What else can go wrong?!!"

This was one question that Evan should *not* have asked.

"What? Why not?" Evan asked the strange voice that appeared out of nowhere a second time. "Why shouldn't I have asked that question? Oh, great. It's *you* again."

"*Huh? What?*" said the Storyteller Guy. "*Are you talking to me?*"

"Of course I'm talking to you!" Evan shouted. "Will you *please* stop interrupting the flow of the story and get on with it?" Even though it was early in the story, Evan was already super annoyed with the Storyteller Guy for all the interruptions. "Hurry up and finish this silly adventure so I can go home!!!"

"*Okay, okay,*" said the Storyteller Guy. "*Let's continue, shall we?*"

(Hole in the Wall continues on the next page.)

(Not this page...the NEXT page.)

(Isn't flipping pages fun? It feels like you're reading this book really fast!!)

Evan was all alone in a strange place, with no idea how to get back home. He was stuck in a strange new world that was weird yet somehow familiar.

Fortunately *(or unfortunately, depending on how much you like the story so far)*, a narrow dirt path curved, winded, zigzagged, and wiggled its way off into the distance, allowing the story to move right along. The path seemed to lead straight into the mountains in the background, which, by the way, were round on top instead of pointy like normal mountains.

"What's the deal with this place?" Evan asked as he began to walk down the dirt path. "Everything here looks strange, and weird, and anti-normal."

This strange new anti-normal world was certainly beautiful, even though it wasn't fully explained to anyone just how strangely beautiful it was. But everything was wrong—or at least different. Nothing looked like it did back home. For starters, all the trees were oddly-shaped, the flowers were all sorts of weird colors, and the grass was bright pink.

"Who ever heard of pink grass, anyway?" Evan said, shaking his head. "Wait a sec—?" Evan took a good look around, thinking that this strange new world looked *exactly* like the painting he'd made in Miss Holly's Little Tykes Pre-School back when he was four years old. It was the first drawing he'd ever made at school. Mother was so proud that she stuck it on the refrigerator with a smiley-face magnet. Evan thought the painting was terrible. Later on, he offered to paint his mother a better one, but she refused.

In his painting, the hills in the background were all perfectly round with heaps of snow on top. There were odd-shaped trees all over the place, the flowers were all weird colors, and the grass was (*you guessed it!*) bright pink.

And, of course, just like in his childish painting, there was a dirt path that curved, winded, zigzagged and wiggled off into the distance.

"This *can't* be my painting?!" Evan asked himself, since there was nobody else around to ask. "Can it??"

There was nothing else to do but keep on walking.

So off he went.

Hours later, Evan threw his arms up into the air and shouted, "What is wrong with this place? It just keeps going!"

going... going...going...GOING...

The sound of his voice echoed, but not in the normal way it did back home. The echo started out small, but then got louder and louder as it came right back again.

"Ridiculous," Evan grumbled, putting his hands on his hips. "Even the echo doesn't work right!" He looked back the way he came and saw that the troll's house, Mr. Jenkinsen's place, was now gone. Missing. Vanished. Disappeared. Ancient history. And when he turned back around again, there was a tall wooden signpost that wasn't there before.

"Where did *that* come from?" Evan stood there scratching his head. The sign, which was about twice as tall as he was, had only one carved wooden arrow on it, and it pointed toward the mountains.

THE CASTLE
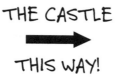
THIS WAY!

"Wait a sec—?" Evan said. "In all the boring old stories I've ever read, the castle doesn't come in until the very end?!"

But this was no boring old story that Evan had ever read before. This was a story about—

"NOT *YOU* AGAIN!" Evan shouted at the strange voice that came out of nowhere for the third time in the same chapter. "Look, *whoever you are*. Can you just hurry up with this weird story so I can go home!?!"

"*Huh? How did—?!*" the Storyteller Guy said, not sure why the hero of his story was talking to him as if he were a real little boy.

"I *am* a real little boy!" Evan shouted at the not-so-bright Storyteller Guy. "Just hurry up and invent someone for me to talk to, will ya?! Besides *you*, weirdo!"

"*Okay, fine,*" said the Storyteller Guy, slightly offended by the hero's harsh tone. "*How about a talking tricycle?*"

"A talking tricycle? Are you *kidding* me?" Evan rolled his eyes, sighed heavily, threw his hands into the air in a disgusted manner, and did all sorts of other cynical-type stuff. "Okay. Fine. Whatever. Just start a new chapter so we can get on with it, okay?"

"*Okie-dokie!*"

Chapter 4

Red the Boy-cycle

Evan turned around and saw a red tricycle. Not just any old red tricycle—*his* red tricycle. The very same one he had back when he was a little kid. The only difference was that this tricycle was alive.

"Hello," said the talking tricycle.

"Um, did you just say *hello*?" Evan asked, knowing good and well that the talking tricycle just said hello, but feeling kind of dumb for talking to an inanimate object that was somehow animated.

Brrring! Brrring! The tricycle person rang its bell, twice, then said, "You betcha!"

"Wow," Evan thought to himself. "That crazy Storyteller Guy wasn't kidding." Out loud, he said, "So you're a talking tricycle? That's pretty weird."

"Nah, not really," the talking bike said through its face, which was painted on the front. "I'm not a tricycle, by the way. I'm a *boy*-cycle. My name is Red."

"It's nice to meet you, Red." Evan looked for a hand to shake, but there wasn't one. So he shook the colorful tassels hanging from Red's handlebars.

"Okay, so now what?" Evan asked.

"Well, first I'm supposed to sing you a song," Red said. "Then we can go to the castle." And before Evan could stop him, Red began to sing.

(Bizarre song begins on the next page.)

Hello, I'm Red.

I'm a talking bike—duh!

I like coffee, and chocolate,

And sugar, and candy,

And I love pizz-a!

I'm your best friend

Cuz' I will always agree,

I'm allergic to peanuts—

YIPPEEEEEE!

If it's good for me, I don't want it

What do I look like? A health nut?!

I love caffeine! And more caffeine!

Brother, can you spare a donut?

Hey, wanna go somewhere? Do sumthin'?

Maybe go downtown?

We could just run around in circles,

Go round! And round! And round!

I'll get you there fast,

Wherever you need to go

Wanna go out for coffee?

Some java? Some joe?

Gimme a good sugar rush,

And I'm faster than a speeding bus!

Um...so....

Hey, come on—

Let's go! Go! Go! Go! Go! GOOOOOOO!

(continued)

Evan thought this was the strangest song he'd ever heard. But Red sang it with such high energy that it was hard not to clap along and tap his foot.

"Okay, *now* we can go to the castle," Red said. "You can ride with me. Hop on!"

"Huh? What? *Now?*" Evan was surprised by the sudden suddenness of it all. He was used to a more evenly paced story, not one that goes straight to the castle.

"Sure, why not?!" Red said. "Didn't you notice the huge wooden signpost right beside you? The one with the arrow pointer thing that says CASTLE THIS WAY."

"Yes, Red, I saw it," Evan said, really wanting to say something cynical, but managing to keep it under control. "Okay, let's go to the stupid castle." Evan didn't like the idea, but saw no other alternative. He hopped on his old bike, which was now a talking bike, and got himself comfortable.

"I just wish *this* story was like all those *other* stories," Evan said. "You know, like where normal stuff happens?"

"But this story isn't like those *other* stories," Red told him, getting ready to zip along the trail. "It's only just begun and you've already encountered a washing machine monster, been dragged through a tunnel into a weird world, then met a mean old troll that looks exactly like your mean old neighbor. Not to mention the fact that you are, right now, having a conversation with a talking tricycle."

"*Boy*-cycle," Evan corrected him.

"Exactly!" Red said, smiling. "Now you're getting it!"

And off they went.

Chapter 5
The Castle
(Which was really called The Town)

The ride only lasted a few seconds. Seven seconds to be exact, but that's really not important to the story.

"Here we are!" Red said, skidding to a halt. The stop was so sudden that Evan went flying clear over the handle bars. He landed in a haystack ten feet away. When he came out a moment later, there was straw stuck in his hair and a needle stuck in his bottom-side.

"OWCH!" Evan cried, pulling out the needle.

"Hey, you found it!" Red cried out. "Good job!"

"Huh? Found what?"

"Never mind," Red said, then shook his front tire just like you'd shake your head. "We're here! I guess we should probably knock. Well, *you* should knock since you're the only one who can make a fist."

Evan and Red were now standing in front of a massive wooden door that was attached to an enormous stone wall. The wall was about twenty feet high and went on forever in either direction. Evan looked to the left and to the right. There was no one else around, and no sound coming from inside.

"Is there anyone inside this dumb place?" Evan asked, pretending like he was thoroughly bored, but really kind of curious to find out what was behind the giant door.

"Only one way to find out!" Red said, looking excited and perhaps a bit hyper.

Evan knocked.

The giant castle door swung open.

Inside was *not* the scene Evan expected to see. It was an entire town filled with all kinds of strange creatures. They were running all over the place, screaming, yelling, and shouting not-so-nice comments at each other. The town was busy and bustling and full of noise, but outside the giant door it was completely silent. However, the moment they set foot inside the place, things got loud, loud, LOUD.

"Hmmm, sound must not travel outside the city walls," Red suggested. "Neat-o!"

"Yeah, neat-o," Evan said, cautiously stepping inside. "Ridiculous is more like it."

The two of them ventured in further. As soon as they were inside, the giant door slammed shut behind them. Now they had no choice but to enter The Town, which, by the way, really *was* named The Town, according to the sign which read like this:

<u>THE TOWN</u>
WELCOME TRAVELLERS!
FROM OTHER WORLDS
AND ELSEWHERE!

There were four main streets. Each one intersected at a place marked "X." The streets were named Tsae Road, Tsew Boulevard, Htron Avenue, and Htuos Street.

"What kind of dumb street names are those?" Evan asked, irritated by the dumbness of it all.

Out of nowhere, a tall, skinny, feathered creature ran past Evan and Red, shouting, "Hurry up and clean!" The silly creature had to swerve to avoid crashing into a group of *other* silly creatures, only to end up crashing into a street light that was inexplicably on during broad daylight.

"It's cleaning day! It's cleaning day!" shouted another bizarre creature, this one short and pudgy.

"I know its Cleaning Day, nincompoop!"

"Clean!"

"Sweep!"

"Dust!"

"Mop!"

"Scrub!"

All kinds of creatures—big, small, furry, hairless, four-legged, six-legged, eight-legged, one hundred-legged—were in a complete panic. They were all shouting about something called Cleaning Day.

Red was wide-eyed and excited, turning his bike-head this way and that, trying to take it all in. Evan, on the other hand, shook his head at the silliness of it all.

"What should we do now?" Red asked.

"Hey, this is *your* world, not mine," Evan said. "You tell me."

"Don't look at me," Red said. "Up until a few minutes ago I didn't even exist! I was just a figment in that weird Storyteller Guy's imagination! Why don't we have a look around? We could take a walk down Tsae Road? Or perhaps Htuos Street?"

"You mean *East* Road and *South* Street?" Evan had already turned his head upside-down to look at the street signs. Once you did this, the signs read properly. At least properly for where Evan came from.

"Hey, you're right!" Red said, turning himself topsy-turvy. "I'll have to make a note of that. Just as soon as I get a notepad, and a pen, and some hands."

Evan and Red decided to explore The Town.

So off they went.

Chapter 6
All Sorts of Strange Creatures

The streets of The Town were lined with all sorts of shops. Mr. B's Boutique, Auntie Smuck's Sweet Shoppe, Barticklemee's Shop-o-rama, and Prissy's Hair Salon just to name a few. There was also Uncle Weaver's Taxidermy, Beverly's Fashion Passion, and Pillburger's Apothecary. There were too many shops to name, and too many busy shop owner creatures to describe. None of them looked even remotely human. But as weird as all the creatures seemed to *him*, Evan figured that he must look equally weird to them.

"CLEAN UP!" all the creatures kept shouting.

"Hurry up! Before Queen Mother gets back!"

At the end of Htuos Street was a steep, grassy hill. *Green* grass this time, not pink. Actually, there was a green grassy hill at the end of each street, road, avenue, or boulevard. But only on the green grassy hill at the end of Htuos Street was anything actually happening—other than cleaning, that is.

Evan and Red stopped here.

There was a big commotion going on at the top of this particular hill. A small furry creature with great long ears stood at the very top. It kind of looked like a rabbit, except that this rabbit seemed to shimmer in the sunlight. Ten other creatures, these ones tall and skinny and pear-shaped, were at the bottom of the hill. They stood perfectly still, formed into a kind of triangular formation.

"KNOCK 'EM DOWN! KNOCK 'EM DOWN!" the shimmering rabbit shouted from the top of the hill.

"KNOCK 'EM DOWN! KNOCK 'EM DOWN!" shouted the tall, skinny, pear-shaped creatures at the bottom of the hill.

Suddenly, the rabbit at the top of the hill began to run really fast. The fuzzy furball began to stumble, then tumble, then roll down the hill. But instead of tumbling down the hill completely out of control, the creature rolled nice and smooth, kind of like a bowling ball. The little guy spun faster and faster. Evan realized the little furball was going to plow right into the poor creatures standing at the bottom of the hill.

"Knock 'em down!"

"Knock 'em down!"

"Knock 'em—"

C
R
A
S
H
!

The shimmering rabbit plowed right into the other creatures with a loud crash. (*See sound effect above!*) The other creatures were launched into the air, scattering all over the place. But not all of them got knocked down. Two still remained.

The bowling ball rabbit shook itself off. Then he marched straight over to Evan and looked up at him furiously.

"What are *you* supposed to be?" the furry creature asked in a snippety tone. Evan couldn't believe it when the creature's entire head disappeared, only to reappear a few seconds later.

"What am *I*?" Evan said, wondering what manner of creature this was. "What are *you*?!" He wasn't sure whether he was more shocked by the creature's rudeness or that different parts of its body kept disappearing at different times. What he had mistaken for shimmering in the sunlight was actually disappearing body parts.

"I asked you first," the rabbit said.

"I happen to be a *person*," Evan told him. He was getting slightly annoyed by this pushy critter. "Actually, I'm a boy."

"A buoy?!" the rabbit said with a mouth that was there, and then wasn't there, and then was there once again. "You mean like a floatation device? Used in the ocean, perhaps? Or a pool? What a silly thing to be."

"No, no, no," Evan said, getting furious with the rude little rabbit. "I am *not* a floatation device, you little furball. I'm a boy. You know, like . . . *like a boy*!"

"Sorry. Never heard of it," the rabbit said. "I, on the other paw, am a Snippet."

"A what?!?"

"No, not a *What*. The Whats are over there," the Snippet said, pointing down Tsew Boulevard to where a group of elderly creatures were standing around, holding their hands up to their ears, shouting, "What?!" and "What did you say?!" and "What was that?!"

"And *now*..." The Snippet turned to look at the two tall, skinny, pear-shaped creatures that were still standing perfectly still. "What would you do in this predicament, buoy? It's the dreaded seven-ten split! You know? Bed posts? Fence posts? Donkey ears?"

"Um, is that a bowling question?" Evan asked, scrunching his eyebrows. "I can't stand bowling. The ball is too heavy, the floor is too slippery, and the shoes look funny and smell funny."

"Well, I will have you know, buoy," the Snippet said, "that Knock 'Em Down —or *bowling* as you call it— happens to be the best game in the world. So there." Turning back to his predicament, the Snippet put a paw to his chin, which both disappeared, first the paw then the chin. Then he began to mumble to himself about how to best knock over the remaining two pins.

"Excuse me, Mr. Snippet," Evan said, feeling quite ignored at the moment. "Could you please tell me who's in charge of this ridiculous place? All these ridiculous stories have a king don't they?"

"Yes, yes, yes," snipped the Snippet. "He's over on the Other Other Hill."

"The Other Hill?" Evan asked, pointing at the hill down at the end of Tsae Road.

"No, no, no. That's the Other Hill. The king is always on top of the *Other* Other Hill. Over there, buoy!!" The Snippet pointed to a completely different hill, which looked exactly like all the others.

"The *Other* Other Hill?" Evan asked. All these ridiculous names were confusing him.

"YES!! Geesh! For a floatation device, you sure do ask a lot of questions," the Snippet said in his snippety tone. "Right over there!"

"Ahh, the *Other* Other Hill," Evan said super sarcastically. "Makes perfect sense to me!"

"What *are* you, some kind of sarcastic echo or something?" the Snippet snapped. "Yes! The *Other* Other

Hill. Right over there, Mr. Snooty-pants! Now get going, will ya? I'M BUSY HERE!"

Evan looked towards the Hill, then the Other Hill, then finally the Other Other Hill. Perched on top of the Other Other Hill was a short, round, smiley-faced man who looked relatively human. The man held a wand in his hand, and was waving it around frantically. This short, stubby person seemed to be conducting the entire town. Evan watched for a moment, realizing that this was *exactly* what was happening.

"Well, buoy?!" the Snippet said. "Are you going to stand here all day or are you going to go talk to the king? I'VE GOT A BOWLING DILEMMA TO DEAL WITH HERE!!" And with that snippety comment, the Snippet turned into a half-visible, half-invisible furball and rolled back up The Hill to take his second shot.

Evan looked to Red for any helpful suggestions.

Brrrring! Brrrring!

"Hey, don't look at me!? This isn't my story," Red said, ringing his bell and giving Evan some kind of weird bicycle-shrug. "Hop on!"

And off they went.

Chapter 7
King Flibbertigibbet

Red screeched to a halt at the bottom of the Other Other Hill. And just to keep things the same, Evan went flying over the handlebars and crashed a second time.

"Sorry!" Red hollered. *Brrring! Brrrring!*

"It's okay," Evan said coming back brushing grass and dirt from his hair and clothes. "I'll be right back. I'm going to go talk to the king up there. You wait here, okay?"

Brrring! Brrring!

"Does that mean yes?" Evan asked his excitable new friend.

Brrring! Brrring!

Evan walked up the Other Other Hill shaking his head, attempting to just roll with it. He could already hear the king shouting orders to the creatures down below.

"Move it, Golliwogs!" the king shouted. "Take a lesson from the Aunts, you lazybones!" The king was yelling at a large group of two-headed creatures, who were sitting on the steps outside one of the shops down below, lazing about, fanning themselves with miniature fans and sipping iced tea.

Evan looked back over his shoulder, recognizing the Golliwogs from their description in the last paragraph. He also recognized the other group of creatures which, he presumed, were the Aunts. These creatures were much smaller than the Golliwogs, with colorful clothing and frizzy grey hair. The Aunts all looked very similar to Evan's Aunt Fredonia, who came over to visit once a month and would always get into a dither whenever there was cleaning to do.

"Don't come crying to *me* if Queen Mother catches you sitting around and decides to turn you into *three*-headed Golliwogs!" the king shouted, never ceasing to wave his wand.

"Oh, wave your wand at someone else, you silly little man!" one of the Golliwogs shouted back. "First we had *no* head, then we had *one* head, and now *two* heads! I don't

59

care if that old Queen turns us into *fifteen*-headed Golliwogs! It's too hot today, and we simply cannot lift a finger."

Suddenly, before any more confusing dialogue, Evan reached the top of the hill.

"Good morning, Evan!" said the king. "How are you today, my inquisitive young friend?"

"Um, how did you know my name?" Evan asked, eyeing the king suspiciously. "And what does *in—qui—si—tive* mean?"

The king was certainly dressed like a royal person. He wore a regal gown, funny pointed shoes, and a great big crown on top of his head. But he had an abnormally round face, a bushy beard, and a smile that went from one incredibly tiny ear to the other. On top of all these bizarre features, he had twinkly blue eyes, huge curly eyebrows, and was extremely short. The man was barely as tall as Evan. He held a wand in his right hand, which he used to conduct the entire town like a symphony.

"As for your first question, I know your name because, um…because it saves a long introduction!" the king said. "You, however, do not know my name. Therefore, and so forth, I will give it to you. Free of charge, of course! My name is King Flibbertigibbet."

Then King Flibbertigibbet started rapping.

I am king! I am king!

I am not a ding-a-ling!

I can't dance, and I sure can't sing

But that's okay, be'cuz I'm king!

King Who? King Huh?

King Where? King Tut?

No, no, no…

I'm King Flibbertigibbet!

That really didn't rhyme

But that's okay…

I conduct The Town

In a superfly way!

I am the king, so hear me roar
And sneeze! And toot! And belch! And snore!
I wave my wand
And so much more!

Queen Mother is the one who's really in charge
But I do stuff, too, if it's not too hard
I'm short, and round, and plump, and cute...
Three cheers for me—Woot! Woot! Woot!

A cow goes moo,
A frog goes ribbit
I am the king...
King Flibbertigibbet!

By the time King Flibbertigibbet finished his terrible rap song, Evan was shaking his head in a most cynical way. Even the king himself looked a little embarrassed about his lame introduction song, and how bad of a rapper he was.

"Sorry about that last part," the king said, showing off his bling. "But there aren't a lot of words that rhyme with Flibbertigibbet, ya know dawg?"

"King Flibbertigibbet? That's a nice simple name," Evan said, not even trying to hide his sarcasm. "So where's your castle?"

"Right there!" King Flibbertigibbet said, pointing at his feet. "Every king needs a castle, even if it isn't quite to scale."

Evan looked to where King Flibbertigibbet was pointing and saw a toy castle exactly like the one he had back home, but had recently deemed himself to mature to play with.

"That's not a real castle," Evan said, unimpressed. "That's just a dumb toy castle."

"Ahh," King Flibbertigibbet said with a toothy grin spreading across his chubby face. "As cheeky in *our* world as you are in your own. How delightful!"

So far, Evan did not like King Flibbertigibbet all that much. The king certainly seemed to know a lot about him, which caused Evan to feel very uncomfortable.

"As for your *second* question, which everyone has probably forgotten by now since you asked it six pages ago—'What does inquisitive mean?'—I can answer that for you, too," the king said. "Or perhaps I can spell it for you? Maybe by writing it on the back of my hand?"

Evan's face suddenly turned white as something that's really white. Somehow, some way, King Flibbertigibbet knew Evan's deep dark secret.

"I have no idea what you're talking about," Evan said, crossing his arms and trying to look innocent. He knew this was a big fat lie, yet he couldn't stop it from spilling out of his mouth. Evan knew *exactly* what King Flibbertigibbet was talking about, but had no idea *how* he knew exactly what he was talking about: *The Spelling Bee competition.*

Regardless of how the king knew about this terrible episode from Evan's past *(which will be explained momentarily)*, it was something that had been bugging him all week…since last Thursday to be exact.

Chapter 7 ½

Cheating on the Thursday Morning Spelling Bee Competition

Every Thursday at Evan's school, Mrs. Towne (*Evan's teacher, in case you weren't sure*) puts on a Spelling Bee competition. Five students get to stand up at the front of the class and have a spell-off. If you spell your word correctly, you go on to the next round. If you *m-i-s-s-p-e-l-l* your word, you have to sit down. Then you don't get to win the big scrumptious chocolate bar that Mrs. Towne hands out for 1st place.

Evan was an *okay* speller, but he had never won the Spelling Bee. Not until last Thursday, that is.

Here's what happened: On Wednesday, the day before the competition, just a few minutes before class was over for the day, Evan *accidently* took a long, long, *very* long look at a certain sheet of paper on Mrs. Towne's desk. Written on this particular sheet of paper were the words she was going to ask during the spelling competition.

Evan walked home that day as quickly as he could, *accidently* repeating the words over and over again so he wouldn't forget them. When he got home, he found each word in the big dictionary that father kept in his study.

Evan tried to memorize the spelling of these difficult words: daffodil, basket, kitchen, handcuffs, serious, and piccolo just to name a few. But he just couldn't make his brain remember them all. That's why he decided the best thing to do would be to write them down on his hand.

On Thursday, when it was Evan's turn to spell a word, he put his hand up to his face *pretending* to be thinking really hard, when he was really just reading the words off the back of his hand. Lucky for him, and for the sake of this long sub-story making sense, nearly every single word Evan had written down on his hand was one of the words Mrs. Towne asked him to spell. The ones he *didn't* know, he just guessed. And just to keep things moving along, let's just say that Evan was a terrific guesser.

Evan ended up winning the contest. He took 1st place, so he got the big scrumptious chocolate bar. He ate the whole thing at recess, right in front of everyone. He didn't share a single bite with any of his classmates.

Afterwards, Evan felt terrible for two reasons. One reason was because of the overload of processed sugar. The second reason was that he knew he had cheated in order to win. All he could do was sit on the merry-go-round with a big, goofy, satisfied grin on his face.

The sugar crash came later.

So did the shame.

Chapter 7 ¾
The Seven Knights of the Week

"I didn't cheat!" Evan shouted at the king, even though he knew very well that cheating was the only reason he'd won the Spelling Bee competition just two days ago.

"No, of course not," King Flibbertigibbet said, giving Evan a curious look. "*You?* Evan Jacob Jacobson? Cheat? No way! Never! Certainly your parents taught you better than that, *hmmmm?*"

Evan stared at his feet.

King Flibbertigibbet waved his wand at a group of rhinoceros-sized creatures who were squatting down and getting ready to do you-know-what right on the fresh cut green grass at the bottom of the Other Other Hill. "Well, if you didn't cheat, like you say, then perhaps you could prove it?"

"Okay, how?" Evan desperately wanted to prove himself innocent.

"Easy! Spell *argle-bargle*," King Flibbertigibbet said as he conducted the rhino-dogs around to the far side of the hill to where a large sign read POTTY FIELD. "Surely a boy who can spell the word daffodil while looking at what's written on the back of his hand can spell something as simple as argle-bargle?"

Evan nervously rubbed his hands together. He didn't even know what an argle-bargle *was* let alone how to spell it.

"No? Well, how about quidnunc?" the king asked, still conducting the chaos down below. "Abibliophobia? Bowyang? Gardyloo?"

Evan shrugged his shoulders.

"None of those?" King Flibbertigibbet said with a know-it-all smirk on his round face. "Surely an excellent speller like yourself shouts *GARDYLOO!!!* every time you throw a bucket of goop out a window?"

Evan shook his head because he knew none of these strange words. What's worse, he was starting to feel guiltier and guiltier about what he'd done. He wished he could go back in time and do the whole thing over again. This time *without* cheating.

"Gaberlunzie? Housegaw? Goobledygook?" The king went on, naming more ridiculous words that no one has ever heard of, but which really are real words. "Oh, come on now. Surely a smart young lad like you must know how to spell floccinaucinihilipilification?"

Evan shook his head.

"Such a pity," the king said. "*And* such a no good, filthy, rotten, sneaky, conniving, scheming, sinister, misguided, imprudent, harsh, thoughtless, uncaring, foolish, pedantic, illegal, plotting, vicious, un-humanitarian, vile, corruptive, disgusting, low-down, uncouth, selfish, nasty, lying little cheater you are! Ho-ho!"

"I—DIDN'T—*CHEAT*!!!" Evan shouted, his face as red as something that's really red. He didn't know who this short, stubby, know-it-all king thought he was, but Evan certainly didn't appreciate being called a liar, or a cheat, or any of those other things in the last paragraph…even if it was all true.

Evan *was* a liar.

Evan *was* a cheater.

He now felt very bad about what he'd done in class. But there was nothing he could do about it right now because the story simply had to move forward.

"There's no sense in denying it, silly child. Of course you cheated!" King Flibbertigibbet smiled and waved his wand with gusto. "And that's why you're going to jail for the rest of your life. Guards, take him away!"

And just like that, with a simple flick of his magical conductor wand, a gaggle of knights came clanging and banging up the hill.

"Forward march-eth!" one of the knights shouted. And march-eth they did. This group of knights was the most uncoordinated bunch of knights-in-shining-armor that Evan had ever seen.

"UP THE HILL!"

"UP THE HILL!"

There were seven knights in total. Each one was wearing battle armor that was either two sizes too big or two sizes too small. Their knees either buckled because of the immense weight, or peeked through the cracks because their armor was too small. Their voices sounded distant and echo-y as they shouted orders at each other. This was because their helmets were on backwards, which was why they couldn't see which way they were going, which was why they were constantly crashing into each other.

While never missing a beat with his conducting, King Flibbertigibbet explained to Evan that the knights marching up the Other Other Hill—the ones who were about to take him to jail for the rest of his life—were the Seven Knights of the Week.

"Their names, of course, are Monday Knight, Tuesday Knight, Wednesday Knight, Thursday Knight, Friday Knight—"

"Yeah, I get it," Evan interrupted. He shook his head at the not-so-cleverness of it all. "Pretty lame."

(If you need to stop here to let the lameness pass, then please do. If not…read on!)

(continued)

"Left, right, left!" Monday Knight shouted, the one leading the brigade.

"Left-right-left?!" Tuesday Knight said. "I thought it was right-left-right?"

"No! It's right-right-left-left, you pea-brain!" Thursday Knight said.

"Oh, shut up and listen to me!" demanded Monday Knight.

"Left! Right! *OWCH*!" shouted Tuesday Knight. "That was my foot! I've been asking you to *please* stop doing that for an extremely very long time!! For hundreds of years!"

"WHAT?!" said Wednesday Knight, his voice tinny and echo-y inside his helmet.

Saturday Knight couldn't make out any of the conversation. "Could you repeat that? I can't hear any of you because my helmet is on backwards!"

"Mine too!" said Friday Knight. "Monday Knight whacked me with that dumb spear of his. Now I can't see where I'm going!"

"And I can't hear what I'm saying!"

"And I can't speak without using exclamation marks!!!"

King Flibbertigibbet conducted and guided the disorganized Knights of the Week up the hill. "Right this way, gentlemen! Just follow the sound of my voice!"

Eventually, the Seven Knights made it to the top of the hill, collapsing in a big pile of armor.

"This is our little cheater right here," King Flibbertigibbet said. Then he passed his wand to the Snippet, the same one Evan had met earlier, who had conveniently appeared out of nowhere. The Snippet stuck its tongue out at Evan, which disappeared and then reappeared. Then the rude little creature took over conducting the town while King Flibbertigibbet spoke to the Seven Knights of the Week.

"This one here is the cheater!" the king said unnecessarily loud. He took a moment to dab his sweaty forehead with a handkerchief. It was the very same kind of handkerchief that Evan's father used to wipe his sweaty forehead whenever he was working in the yard, mowing the lawn, or tinkering with his piece-of-junk car.

"I can't stand cheaters!" shouted a knight from somewhere at the bottom of the pile.

"Yeah, me either!"

"Yeah, me neither!"

"Oh, be quiet! You can't even *spell* cheater!"

"Can too! C—h—e—e—t—"

"INCORRECT!"

"Gentlemen, gentlemen!" the king interrupted. "I know you are all terrific word-spellers, able to do so *without* cheating. This one here, however—" King Flibbertigibbet pointed at Evan. "He is not as noble as you, since he is a disreputable spelling bee cheater. Therefore, and furthermore, I command that you take him down to the jailhouse and lock him up for the rest of his life, plus one extra year for every word he cheated on."

The Seven Knights of the Week all saluted the king, saying, "Aye, aye, Captain!" like they were a bunch of sailors or something.

"Okay then," the king said. "Off you go!" Then he took his wand back from the Snippet and continued to conduct all the creatures down below. "You heard me, off to jail!"

"OFF TO JAIL!" the knights all shouted. They grabbed a hold of Evan and dragged him down the hill and off to jail, shouting in unison: "Off to jail! Off to jail!" until it got very tiresome.

Chapter 8
Off to Jail

"OFF TO JAIL!"

"OFF TO JAIL!"

"OFF TO JAIL!" The Seven Knights of the Week continued to chant right into the next chapter.

"OFF TO JAIL! OFF TO JAIL!"

The knights dragged Evan down to the bottom of the Other Other Hill, through the crowded streets, then over to a brick building marked JAILHOUSE.

As Evan was shoved up the front steps, he couldn't help but notice the long slimy snake working on the outside of the building. This curious snake was standing on a ladder, which reminded Evan of his favorite board game when he was a little kid—oddly, he couldn't recall the name of that game right now.

"Eww," Monday Knight said. "I hate snakes."

The snake creature had a wispy moustache, a red beret tilted to one side, tiny black sunglasses, and was holding a paintbrush in one tiny snake-hand and a paint pallet in the other. The snake-artist was adding something extra to the sign that hung above the front entrance.

Now it read like this:

JAILHOUSE
for spelling bee cheaters

"Until he rots!" Monday Knight said.

"Yeah! Until he rots!" echoed Friday Knight.

"UNTIL HE ROTS!" the others chimed in.

"Yeah! Or until next Saturday!" Sunday Knight said from way in the back somewhere. "That's when we'll have to let him out so we can tidy up the cell again for Cleaning Day!"

"*Yeah!!!*" the others cried together.

"UNTIL NEXT WEEK!"

"UNTIL NEXT WEEK!"

"UNTIL NEXT WEEK!"

"Oh, be quiet, all of you!" Monday Knight said. Then he whacked each of them on the head with his javelin. "We've got a prisoner to put in jail for the rest of his life. After that, we've got cleaning to do! March! March! March!"

"March?!" Sunday Knight asked quietly. "I thought it was June?"

Chapter 9

Jailhouse Poetry

Jail is boring

It has bad food,

Jail puts me in a terrible mood.

Jail is quiet, there's no one to talk to,

Jail is smelly, and there's nothing to do.

Jail is awful

Jail is dumb

Jail is not fun

Okay, I'm done.

Poem by Evan Jacob Jacobson

(Written in jail)

Chapter 10
Red to the Rescue

Miraculously, barely five minutes into his stay in jail—
which was just long enough to write that terrible poem—
the entire back wall of Evan's cell came crumbling down.

C   A   H

   R   S   !

Parked just outside was Red the Boy-cycle. Red looked
excited, hyper, and a whole lotta revved up. There was a
heavy rope with a hook attached to his handlebars, which
were also sort of his ears.

Incredibly, even though he didn't have any hands, Red
was somehow able to toss the heavy rope up towards the
window *and* get the hook to land perfectly on one of the

bars. Conveniently, he also possessed super-strength to pull down the wall.

"Hi, Evan!" Red said. His bicycle body wiggled and jiggled with excitement. Red was certainly glad to see that his new friend was okay. "Thought you could use a helping, uh…"

"A helping handlebar?" Evan suggested.

Brrring! Brrring! Brrring! Brrring! Brrring! Brrring! Brrring!

"Red, are you okay?" Evan asked. "You look a little, um—how should I put this gently…insane?"

While Evan had been talking with King Flibbertigibbet on top of the Other Other Hill just a few pages ago, Red had wheeled himself into Whole Lotta Lattes coffee shop down on Htron Avenue, where he ordered eleven cups of straight black coffee, a half-caf skinny mocha with cinnamon, a triple-shot non-fat latte with whipped cream, a scone, and a quadruple espresso. But as to where he found the rope and the grappling hook, nobody knows.

This was how Red helped Evan escape from jail.

Moving right along!

Chapter 11
The Three Quests

Once Evan escaped from jail, he got on Red's back, and they zoomed back up to the top of the Other Other Hill.

"A-ha! Out of jail already?" King Flibbertigibbet asked. "How delightful!" He was still conducting The Town, keeping all the creatures in check and cleaning away like mad before Queen Mother's arrival.

Without saying a word, Evan snatched the wand right out of the king's right hand, right then, and rightly so.

"GIVE THAT BACK!" King Flibbertigibbet demanded. "QUICKLY, YOU WORD-CHEATER! THE CREATURES WILL DESTROY THE TOWN IF I DON'T KEEP THEM IN HARMONIOUS HARMONY!"

"Not until you tell me how I can get home," Evan said. "Tell me, and then you can have your silly baton back."

"It is not a *baton*! It's a conductor's wand!" the king screamed. "And I want it back. Now! Gimme-gimme-gimme!" The king then proceeded to have a full-blown temper tantrum. It was quite ridiculous to watch a grown man flopping around, wailing like a kid who dropped his ice cream cone. But it was also very entertaining. The king wailed and moaned, stomped his feet, did a couple summersaults, even a springy backflip.

"Are you quite finished, dear sir?" Evan asked, momentarily sounding very sophisticated for a kid. He was holding the wand behind his back.

"Yes, I believe so," King Flibbertigibbet said, then took a few deep breaths to calm down. There was dirt all over his gown and clumps of grass stuck in his crown from the summersaults.

"You'd better hurry up and tell me how I can get home," Evan said. "Otherwise, it looks like your town will get smashed into bits and pieces."

Down below things were not going so well. King

Flibbertigibbet tried conducting everyone by just using his hand. When that didn't work, he pulled on Evan's pant leg and begged for his magical wand back.

"Okay, okay!" the king said. "I give up! You win! I'll do whatever you want. Just give me back my wand!" The Town was going berserk without their conductor to guide them. All the creatures were smashing, crashing, thrashing and bashing everything in sight. King Flibbertigibbet hummed and hawed as he tried to come up with something to tell Evan.

"How about…you could, um…" The king desperately tried to think of some way to send Evan home just so he could get his wand back——even if this meant *lying* to the boy, which went against his whole lecture about cheating during the Spelling Bee.

"Um…um…um…" The king finally thought of something. "Voila! Eureka, Kansas! I've got it! The Three Quests! You could complete the Three Quests!"

"The what?" Evan asked.

"The Three Quests, silly child!" King Flibbertigibbet shouted, still in a complete panic as he watched his town being destroyed by its own townsfolk. "Everyone knows about the Three Quests!"

"I don't," Evan told him.

"Well, I'll explain it to you if you *stop interrupting me*!?"

"Sorry."

"*There!*" the king shouted, pointing at Evan with one hand while ripping out a chunk of his hair with the other. "You did it again just now!"

Evan saw that this could take a very long time, so he zipped his lip and let King Flibbertigibbet explain to him all about the Three Quests.

"Well then," the king began. "There are three quests, you see? And these three quests are called—"

"The Three Quests?" Evan said, unable to resist.

"Don't push your luck, wand-stealer!" King Flibbertigibbet snapped. "*Yes*, Mr. Smarty-pants. They are called the Three Quests. And you must complete all three of these quests before Queen Mother gets back. If you don't then you'll be in big, BIG trouble, buster!"

"Big, BIG trouble, eh?" Evan repeated.

"Is there an *echo* in here or what?! Yes, you annoying

little repeater! Big, *big* trouble!" The king steadied himself. "Now, as I have been *trying* to explain, you have three chances to bring back the…" The king scratched his head. "What was that thingamajig you broke back in your world?"

"The unicorn?"

"Yes, yes. That's it! You have three chances to bring back the unicorn." The king gave Evan a big smile, trying to distract him. Then he tried to grab the wand from behind Evan's back. Evan stopped him by simply pushing his hand against King Flibbertigibbet's sweaty forehead.

"The unicorn?" Evan asked, a little surprised by this new plot development. "I have to bring back a unicorn?"

Breaking mother's favorite crystal unicorn figurine was what brought Evan to this upside-down world in the first place. It didn't make sense that he had to find another unicorn just so he could go back home? Come to think of it, nothing so far had made much sense, so Evan decided that this sounded perfectly reasonable. That's why he agreed to do the Three Quests so that he could finally go home.

"Agreed," Evan said, handing back the wand.

"Agreed," King Flibbertigibbet said. He took his wand back and conducted the town at a furious pace. After a few tense moments, everything went back to normal...or as normal as things could be for such a strange place.

"So? Where do I go?" Evan asked.

"What do you mean *Where do I go?*" King Flibbertigibbet said, acting as if Evan had just asked the dumbest question ever. "There are only three places you *can* go in our world, pea-brain! Geesh! For a cynical know-it-all little boy, you certainly don't know much about the things you ought to know, you know?"

"No."

"Exactly!" the king said. "Listen, smart aleck—"

"My name is Evan."

"I know that!!" the king shouted in an irately irate fashion. "Stop being so smart-alecky!" After regaining his composure, the king said, "You did something wrong back in *your* world, so that's why you ended up here in *our* world. That is how all cynical know-it-all little brats end up here. They break something, or steal something, or get caught

cheating, or all three."

"Fine," Evan said, getting fed up with the king's attitude. "But you still haven't told me where to go? Be quick about it, okay? I want to get these silly quests over with so I can go home."

"Ho-ho! Shows what *you* know, you cynical little know-nothing." King Flibbertigibbet held his tiny nose up in the air. "As I told you a moment ago, there are only three places you *can* go in our world: The Forest of Flatulence, the Odiferous Underground, and the Sea of Wonk."

"The Sea of *what?*"

"The Sea of Wonk," the king repeated. "You know—Wonk? Milk? Two percent?"

Evan knew exactly what King Flibbertigibbet was talking about, which unfortunately would not be explained until much later in the story.

"Whatever," Evan said, getting back on top of Red, who looked excited and ready to begin a quest—*three* quests. "Just point us in the right direction, okay? I'll figure the rest out by myself. Some help *you* are, King Flicketybooger."

"*KING FLIBBERTIGIBBET*!!!" the king yelled. "Just pick a direction and *go*," he said, pointing every which way. "Now get out of my sight. I have a town to conduct!" With a flick of his wrist, the front door opened up.

Evan and Red left quickly. They raced down the Other Other Hill, through the town, past all the crazy cleaning creatures, then out the front gate. The doors slammed shut behind them and everything got very quiet just like before.

"Thank goodness that's over," Evan said.

Brrring! Brrring!

"Now what do we do?" Red asked.

The two of them were all alone, still unsure about which way to go. So just to keep things moving along, a tall wooden signpost magically appeared out of nowhere. It had a single arrow on it (*just like before*), which pointed them in the right direction (*also just like before*).

The sign read like this:

FOREST OF FLATULENCE

➡

THIS WAY

And off they went.

Chapter 12
The Forest of Flatulence

Evan and Red sped off down the dirt path. To save time, and paper, within a few minutes they passed their first road sign. Just a few feet after that, they reached a second road sign, and another, and another.

The signs all read like this:

FOREST OF FLATULENCE 10,000 YARDS

FOREST OF FLATULENCE 9,999 YARDS

FOREST OF FLATULENCE 9,998 YARDS

FOREST OF FLATULENCE 9,997 YARDS

Fortunately, Red was still hopped-up on caffeine, so they were able to arrive at the forest in no time at all. And just to keep things consistent, Evan went flying over the handlebars when Red skidded to a stop, and landed on his bottom-side right in front of a door.

A big red door.

It made absolutely no sense to have a big red door right in the middle of a ten-foot-tall hedge, but there it was, along with the previously mentioned hedge. The hedge went on forever in either direction. There was nothing else around. It was just them, the path, the terribly drawn mountains in the background, the tall hedge that went on forever, and the big red door.

"This must be the place," Evan said, coming to an ingenious conclusion. "Let's get this first quest over with, shall we?"

"Uh-oh!" Red said, ringing his bell. By wiggling his front tire, he gestured towards another sign that suddenly popped up out of nowhere, possibly while their heads were turned.

This new sign read as follows:

Welcome to the Forest of Flatulence!
ENTER HERE
(One at a time, please!)

Right beside the ENTER HERE sign was another sign. This one was a life-sized cardboard cutout of King Flibbertigibbet, grinning ear to ear, holding his hand above his fat head. There was a large round cartoon dialogue bubble hanging above his large round head. Inside the speech bubble were the following words:

YOU MUST BE *AT LEAST*
THIS TALL TO ENTER!

Evan put his back up against the cardboard picture of the king. He sighed a sigh of great relief when he discovered that he was just tall enough to meet the height requirement. Unfortunately, Red wasn't even close.

"Aw, gee golly gosh!" Red said, cussing like it was the 1930s. "I'm way too short. I guess you'll have to go in by yourself!" *Brrring! Brrring!*

Evan didn't like the idea of going in alone, but it looked like there was no other choice.

Knock! Knock! Knock!

Evan knocked three times, in case the above sentence was unclear. The big red door swung open. Once again, there was no noise coming from inside. What's worse, Evan thought it looked really spooky in there, and kind of scary.

Evan gave Red a fearful look.

Brrring! Brrring! Red rang his bell in hopes that it would somehow calm Evan's nerves. It didn't help.

"See you soon, Red," Evan said from inside the doorway. "I hope…" The moment Evan stepped through the archway, the big red door slammed shut. Only then did the forest come alive with all sorts of forest-y noises, like birds and crickets, hooting owls, snapping twigs, and stuff like that.

"There's nothing to be scared of," Evan told himself. "Nope, there's absolutely nothing to be scared of in here. You're a big kid now. There is absolutely nothing to be scared—"

"Rrrrrrrrrrrr," came a deep growl.

Evan spun around to face the terrible beast that was right behind him. But there was nothing there.

Correction: there was nothing there *except* for a log. And this particular log had a mouth, a nose, and big blue eyes that were staring right at him.

Evan blinked . . . so did the log.

Evan twitched his nose . . . so did the log.

Evan pretended to *pick* his nose...but the log couldn't because it didn't have hands. Instead, the log rolled forward, causing Evan to scream.

"Oh, quit your screaming, you big baby," the log said. "You'll set the Danes on us if you don't pipe down! *Shhhh*!!"

Evan couldn't believe his eyes *or* his ears. "Are you a talking log?" he asked, knowing good and well that the log just spoke to him.

"Yes, I'm a talking log," said the talking log. "I should think that it would be painfully obvious since I am talking to you *right now*."

"Wonderful," Evan said, shaking his head. "So far I've met a grumpy troll that looks just like my grumpy neighbor, a coffee drinking boy-cycle, all sorts of weird creatures cleaning up their weird town, a whiny king *conducting* the weird creatures cleaning up the town, and now a talking log. *Can things possibly get any worse?!!*"

Then things got worse.

Bump began to sing.

(Terrible singing starting soon.)

I'm Bump, I'm Bump, I'm Bump

Some will say I'm a grump

I don't have arms,

Or legs, or hair

And I certainly don't have a rump!

I talk and roll,

And roll and talk

Faster than most people walk

All with no feet!

Hey, isn't that neat?

No, I don't want a pair of socks!

I'm smart and funny and clever,

But please don't knit me a sweater

I just couldn't bear it!

I couldn't possibly wear it!

Surely, being a Log must be better?!

I am a Talking Log

Not a talking dog or a frog,

Cuz' that wouldn't make any sense—

And best of all . . .

I don't have to wear pants!

(continued)

Evan was not impressed. "That last part didn't even rhyme. You can't rhyme the word *sense* with the word *pants*. Everyone knows that."

"True enough," Bump said. "But *I* didn't write that awful song. I merely have to sing it whenever I meet somebody new. And *you*, cynical little boy, are somebody new. Now what exactly are you doing here? This is not a place for children. There are very scary things in this forest."

"I have to find something, Mr. Log, sir," Evan told him, assuming that the talking log was a male and not a female."

"As I already told you in that ridiculous song just now," said the talking log, "my name is Bump. Pleased to meet you."

"Hi, Bump," Evan said, looking for a hand to shake, but talking logs don't have hands. Instead he patted Bump on the head. "Pleased to meet you, too."

"Now, what exactly is this 'something' that you must find?" Bump asked, rolling closer to Evan. Evan couldn't help but notice that each time Bump rolled over he would squash his own face into the dirt, causing him to say "OWCH!" But Evan had seen many strange things already, so he just did what any rational person would do... he rolled with it.

"I have to find a unicorn," Evan said, looking around the forest. He couldn't be sure, but he was pretty sure he saw several tiny heads poking out from behind the trees. Tiny *blue* heads to be exact. Looking again, he saw nothing but trees, trees, and more trees. It also occurred to Evan that although the Forest of Flatulence was quite dense, it did not smell nearly as bad as he expected it to.

"The u-u-u...the u-u-u—" Bump stuttered as if saying the word 'unicorn' was the most difficult thing in the world. "The u-u-u...u-u-u—"

"Unicorn," Evan repeated. "Why do you stutter when trying to say the word unicorn?"

"SHHHHHH!" Bump hissed, looking around nervously. "Be quiet or they'll hear you! Us! Whatever!"

"*They*? They who? Who'll hear me? Us? Whatever?" Evan looked around the empty forest. As far as he could tell, he and his new friend, Bump, were the only two people—living things—in the whole forest.

"The Danes, you fool!" Bump said. His bright blue eyes were wide with fear. "The Danes will hear you! Us! Whatever!"

"You mean, like…Danish people?" Evan asked, not sure what the big deal was. He'd never met anyone from Denmark before, but he was sure they'd be very nice. "Don't they wear wooden shoes?"

"No, no, no, no—*OWCH!*" Bump cried as he rolled over his face. "The Swedes wear—*OWCH!*—wooden shoes. The Nords have—*OWCH!*—trolls on the brain. And the Danes are very happy. A little *too* happy, if you ask me. Ever since they won that—*OWCH!*—Happiest Country in the World competition a few years ago, they've been—*OWCH!*—completely unbearable."

Evan had no idea what Bump was talking about. Either way, the two of them began to walk *(roll)* through the forest. As they continued to move along the trail, Bump seemed to know that something was up, though he refused to say what. He just kept sniffing the air, thinking that Evan didn't notice.

Sniff! Sniff!

"Why do you keep sniffing the air?" Evan asked as they rounded another curve and headed deeper into the forest.

"Oh, no reason," Bump said, then sniffed the air again.

Soon, a raunchy, odiferous odor filled the air.

"Hey, Bump?" Evan asked, pulling his shirt up over his nose. "Did you just, um…" He didn't want to embarrass his new friend or anything, but it smelled like someone tooted. Evan didn't toot, so he decided it must've been Bump.

Suddenly, they were ambushed.

Actually, they were questioned first, and *then* they were ambushed.

"HALT!" shouted the tiny blue creature that suddenly jumped out from behind a tree. The tiny blue critter had fierce eyes, a spiky red Mohawk, and smelled awful.

Evan and Bump halted.

"Stop right there!" the stinky creature demanded. "I am Captain One-Cheek-Sneak, leader of the Fartleks!

Who are you?! *What* are you?! Why are you trespassing in our forest?!"

"Oh no," Bump groaned. "They've found us." Bump started rolling all over the place, looking for somewhere to hide, but it was too late. Hundreds of tiny blue creatures popped out of their hiding spots and surrounded them.

"Um, did you just say that you're a *Fart-lick*?" Evan asked. "Because if you did, that's the worst name I've ever heard." Evan started giggling. This further enraged Captain One-Cheek-Sneak.

"I said *Fartlek*," the tiny blue creature shouted. "Not fart-lick! Fartlek! Fartlek! FARTLEK! You know, like the excruciatingly intense workout the Swedes came up with? Ring any bells?"

Evan shook his head.

All of a sudden, the entire mob of Fartleks began to exercise while singing a really annoying song which begins on the next page.

One, and two, and three, and four
Fartleks can run and jump and more
Five, and six, and seven, and eight
Fartleks can hop and skip and skate

Nine, and ten, and eleven, and twelve
Don't stop now, and don't slow down
Squats! Sit-ups! And jumping jacks
Clean-and-jerk and split your pants

Thirteen, fourteen, fifteen, sixteen
Thank the Swedes for this silly routine
Seventeen, eighteen, nineteen, twenty
You want more rhymes? We've got plenty

Twenty-one, twenty-two, twenty-three, twenty-four
We can count and rhyme lots more
Twenty-five, twenty-six, twenty-seven, twenty-eight—

"STOOOOOP!" Evan cried. His hands were clamped over his ears to drown out the awful song. "That's the worst song I've ever heard! It just keeps going and going!"

Never in their entire history had the Fartleks ever been interrupted while singing their introduction song.

"We didn't even make it to one thousand!" yelled Captain One-Cheek-Sneak, who was so mad that he tooted. Then he started exercising frantically, doing jumping jacks and screaming at the other Fartleks in a high-pitched squeaky voice. He yelled at his commanding officer, Sergeant Silent-But-Deadly, to do something.

"I've got it! We will take you to the happy people!" Sergeant Silent-But-Deadly said. "They'll know what to do with you, you...annoying annoyers!!"

"NO!" Bump screamed. "NOT THE DANES?!!"

"Yes, the Danes!" shouted Captain One-Cheek-Sneak, and then he laughed one of those evil bad guy laughs. "Move it, talking log! We're taking you to see the Danes! Immediately! Right now! Before this chapter drags on any longer! MUSH! MUSH! MUSH!"

And off they mushed.

Chapter 13
The Dancing Danes

Evan, Bump, and the mob of Fartleks walked through the Forest of Flatulence for a very, very, very long time. They walked for so long that it began to get dark. They walked for such an entirely too long time that Evan's feet began to get sore. So did Bump's face from rolling over it so many times.

But the walking wasn't the worst part. The worst part, by far, was the stinky stench of the Fartleks. All the little blue guys were in terrific shape from all the exercise, but boy-oh-boy did they have terrible gas. Evan had no idea what tiny blue Mohawk creatures eat, but if he had to guess, he would've guessed they ate a lot of beans.

Finally, after entirely too much flatulation, they came to a clearing in the woods. It was about time they reached *somewhere* since even the Storyteller Guy was getting grossed out by all the stinky toots. The Fartleks seemed to each have a trumpet attached to their bottom.

"Here we are!" cried Captain One-Cheek-Sneak. "Company...*halt*!"

The group stopped right in the middle of a huge campground. Evan and Bump saw a big campfire, with a bunch of normal-looking people dancing around the fire and having a wonderful time. There was even a band playing some very upbeat music.

"Are those the Danes?" Evan whispered to Bump. Bump opened his eyes briefly, only to slam them shut again. The poor guy was absolutely terrified for some reason.

"Yes!" Bump whispered. "Evan, you've got to do something!!"

Evan thought the Danes looked pretty normal. They were just plain old regular-looking men and women. Each one had their own individual characteristics, yet simultaneously looked exactly alike. One was fat, one was skinny. One was tall, one was short. One was bald, one was hairy. One was old, one was young. One had long hair, one had short hair. One had a moustache, one had a beard. One was pretty, one was pretty ugly.

The Danes all wore red jumpsuits with a white stripe down the side. Most of them were waving a small Danish flag. They were also smiling—a lot.

"What's so terrible about the Danes?" Evan asked. The whole time they'd been walking through the forest, Bump had gone on and on about how awful the Danes were. Evan imagined they'd be big, ugly, horrible creatures ready to eat him up and spit out the bones.

This wasn't the case at all.

The Danes looked perfectly normal. Well, normal except for the non-stop dancing, the constant flag-waving, the matching jump suits, and the huge goofy grins that never left their happy faces. Other than *those* few peculiar things, the Danes all looked perfectly normal.

"You'll see," Bump said. "Just wait a few pages."

Evan thought that Bump was overreacting. One thing was for sure: the Danes sure knew how to have a good time!

Evan quickly found himself tapping his foot to the music. The band was busy playing drums, guitar, trumpet, accordion, harmonica, violin, tuba, organ, cello, flute, piccolo, piano, tambourine, bongos, triangle, nose-harp, and many other music making things that you, the reader, can think of because the Storyteller Guy has exhausted his limited knowledge of musical instruments.

And the most incredible part was that even though the band was rocking out on their instruments, they never stopped dancing.

"Wait here!" said Captain One-Cheek-Sneak. Then he stomped over to the most noticeable Dane, the Tall Dane, who was dancing next to the campfire while roasting a marshmallow.

After a brief conversation that doesn't need explaining, Evan overheard the Tall Dane say to Captain One-Cheek-Sneak, "YA! BREENG DEM O'VAH! KVIKLY, PLEEZ! BEEFOR ZA SONG IZ O'VAH!"

And while this was going on, Bump kept bumping up against Evan's leg, saying, "Do something! Quick! Get us out of here!!"

"What? Why?" Evan asked. "They look like extremely civilized people."

"Last time I was here they made me . . ."

Before Evan could find out what the Danes made Bump do the last time, Captain One-Cheek-Sneak returned. He ordered Evan and Bump to march forward, and march forward they did.

"Move it, you two!" shouted the Fartlek's leader, prodding Evan and Bump with his miniature spear. "The leader of the Danes will know what to do with you. That's him over there, the Tall Dane. They call him that because he's very, very—"

"Tall?" Evan said with a smirk on his face.

"*Silence!*" the Fartlek demanded. "You're in for it now, annoying sentence finisher!"

The next thing they knew, Evan and Bump were being introduced to the Tall Dane. When they got up close, Evan realized that this Danish fellow looked exactly like Mr. Jørgensen, the tallest teacher at Lincoln Elementary School. In fact, he couldn't be sure, but Evan was *pretty sure* that in real life Mr. Jørgensen was actually from Denmark.

"VELL, HELLO TALKING LOG!" said the Tall Dane who looked just like Mr. Jørgensen. He reached down and patted Bump on the head, never missing a beat with his weird dancing routine. "I REMEMBER YOU! HOW ARE YOU? AND HELLO TALKING BOY! COME UN JOIN US, YA! VEE ARE DANCING!"

"Yes, I can see that," Evan said.

"BUT VHUT'S YOUR NAME?" the Tall Dane asked as he did several high-kicks.

"But *what?*" Evan shouted, struggling to be heard over the loud music.

"VHUT'S ZAT YOU ZAY?! JOR NAME IZ BUTT-VHUT?" said another Dane, the Short Dane, who'd poked his head around the fire to see what was going on. "VHUT A ZILLY NAME YOU 'AVE, BUTT-VHUT! HA-HA-HA-HA!"

"HEY, GUYZ! GET ZA LOAD OF DIZ!?" called the Skinny Dane. "ZA LEETLE BOYZ NAME IZ BUTT-VHUT!!!"

The Danes all started laughing. So did the Fartleks. Bump giggled too, but then he was suddenly grabbed by the Young Dane and was soon being spun around in a crazy dance.

"No, no, no!" Evan said, getting mad because he was being made fun of. "My name isn't Butt-Vhut."

"VELL, ZEN?" asked the Pretty Dane. "VHUT *IZ* IT?"

"Well, if you stop dancing for *two seconds* then maybe I can tell you," Evan said, crossing his arms. The Dancing Danes were starting to get on his nerves.

"SHTOP DANCING?!" the Tall Dane said. A curious look spread across his happy, smiling face. "VYE VOULD VEE EVER SHTOP DANCING, YOU ZILLY BOY?! VEE ARE ZA DANES! AND VEE DANCE! DEEDN'T YOU KNOW ZAT VEE VURE VOTED 'APPIEST COUNTRY IN ZA VURLD?"

The Danes all gave a tremendous cheer.

"Um, no, I didn't know that," Evan said, already beginning to think the Danes were a little *too* happy. "Vye vould I know zat?" Evan said. "I mean, *why* would I know that?"

The Danes excitement and their happiness was very contagious. The Fartleks were already dancing all around the trees, the fire, even *in* the fire, since it turns out that the tiny blue creatures with the funny name were fireproof.

"How strange," Evan said, suddenly finding himself compelled to shake his little tushy. "I didn't even know I could do the boogie-woogie!"

121

(Six and a half hours later...)

The Danes were *still* dancing. So were the Fartleks. So was Evan. So was Bump, even though he didn't have legs. The Danes would take turns with Bump the talking log, spinning him round and round, then passing him along to the next person.

Everyone was having a wonderful time. This included the cynical little boy who used to think that dancing was only for adults. The only problem was that Evan's legs, feet, and arms were very tired from all the dancing. When he tried to tell the Danes that he needed to stop and rest for a while…well, that's when Evan clued in to what was wrong with them: the Danes *never* stopped being happy, and *never* stopped dancing.

"YOU VANT TO TAKE ZA REST NOW?" asked one of the Danes when Evan tried to sit down and have a quick rest. "BUTT VEE JUZT SHTARTED A NEW SONG!"

"Just a quick rest," Evan said, huffing and puffing. "Just a little sit-down—WHOA!" Before he could sit down, one of the Danes dragged him off to dance some more. They kept dancing and dancing and dancing and dancing and dancing and dancing and dancing and

dancing and dancing and dancing and dancing and
dancing and dancing and dancing and dancing and
dancing and dancing and dancing and dancing and
dancing and dancing and dancing and dancing and
dancing and dancing and dancing and dancing and
dancing and dancing and dancing and dancing and
dancing and dancing until it got very repetitive and
annoying and took up almost half a page.

"STOP!" Evan cried. "I can't have a good time
anymore! I have to find—" Whoosh! Another partner
change. "I 'ave to vind za—" Whoosh! Another partner
change. *Whoosh! Whoosh! Whoosh!*

Evan got spun around so many times that he felt like
he was going to be sick. Eventually, Evan wound up
dancing with Bump. Evan kicked his feet out to the side,
wiggled his bottom, and spun Bump around while
pretending to have a wonderful time. What he was really
trying to do was have a secret conversation with his friend
so they could plan their escape.

"*Now* do you see why the Danes are so dangerous?!"
Bump whispered, looking tired and worn out and dizzy
from being spun around so much. "*Now* do you see what's

wrong with them? They *never* stop being happy! Ever!! They've been unbearably chipper ever since they won that Happiest Country in the World contest!"

"I still have to find za unicorn!" Evan shouted over the blaring music. "I mean...I have to find *the* unicorn! I have to find the unicorn so I can go home!"

"VHUT'S ZAT, BUTT-VHUT?" the Tall Dane asked, sneaking up behind them and listening in on their conversation. The Dane who looked just like Mr. Jørgensen was practically sleep-dancing. His eyes were almost completely shut, but his feet still moved swiftly.

"I have to get home, Mr. Dane, sir!" Evan shouted, twirling Bump around for a do-si-do. "My father is waiting for me. I have to finish doing my chores! But I can't go home unless I find the unicorn!"

"VHUT DID YOU SAY, BUTT-VHUT?" the Tall Dane shouted, cupping a hand to his ear. "VEE CAN'T 'EAR YOU BECUZ ZA MUZIC EES TOO LOWD! AND ALZO BECUZ MY EYES ARE CLOZED! YA! EET'S NAP TIME *AND* ZA DANCING TIME!"

"I 'ave to vind zee unicorn!" Evan told him, dancing around in circles with Bump. "I mean…I have to find the unicorn!"

"ZA UNI-CORN?!" the Skinny Dane said, coming over to warm himself by the fire. "ZA GREAT GOLDEN UNI-CORN? VYE DEEDN'T YOU ZAY ZO?!"

Evan watched him dance over to the band, put in a song request, then dance off somewhere else just out of sight. For sheer convenience, he came back very quickly holding something in his hand.

"VAKE UP, YOU ZILLY GOOSE!" the Skinny Dane said to the Tall Dane. He had to shake him pretty hard to wake him up. Then he handed him a golden ear of corn.

"HUH? VHUT?" the Tall Dane said, snapping awake. The Skinny Dane exchanged a few words with the leader of the Danes, then he danced over to the snack table to get some punch.

"AHH! YOU NEED ZA UNI-CORN?" the Tall Dane said, coming over and dancing alongside Evan and Bump once more. "VYE DEEDN'T YOU SAY ZO?"

126

"I *deed* say so," Evan told him very non-politely. "But you *deedn't* hear me because you were dancing with your eyes closed!"

"VELL? 'ERE EET IZ!" the Tall Dane said, holding up the dried ear of corn. "EET'S ZA CORN! *AND* EET'S ZA UNI! YA! EET'S ZA UNI-CORN!"

"Um, no it's not," Evan said. "That's just a stupid ear of corn." But the more he thought about it, the more he could see that *technically* the Dane was right. It *was* corn. And it was also a *uni*. It was a uni-corn.

"Absolutely ridiculous," Evan said, shaking his head at the nerve of the Storyteller Guy. "I guess I'll just have to roll with it!"

However, Evan didn't think for one second that this whole 'uni-corn' bit would fool King Flibbertigibbet. The king may be annoying, and immature, and he made his living by waving a baton in the air, but he was still reasonably clever. Even if the king *did* fall for it, the one person that Evan was really worried about was the one called Queen Mother. Even the king himself said during his terrible rap song that *she* was really the real ruler who's really in charge. Queen Mother didn't sound like someone who would be fooled by a dumb old hunk of corn, even if it was glorious and golden.

"ZURE EET'S ZA CORN!" hollered the Chubby Dane, over by the fire, roasting fifteen marshmallows at a time. "EET'S ZA CORN! *AND* EETZ ZA UNI! EET'S ZA UNI-CORN!"

"Yeah, I heard that part already," Evan said, still dancing, still plotting his escape.

Then there was trouble.

Chapter 14
Evan and Bump Escape
(The G-rated version)

"Run for it!" Evan shouted.

"I can't *run*, remember?!" Bump shouted back. "I'm a log!!"

"Okay, then roll for it!" Evan hollered.

And off they rolled.

INTERRUPTION:

The Storyteller Guy is sincerely sorry for this interruption, but thought that you, the reader, were probably getting too scared back there. Hey, nonstop line-dancing is enough to frighten anyone.

Therefore, I created the alternate escape scene which you just read. If, however, you dare to read what really happened, then proceed to Chapter 15, the R-rated version. If you are worried that it may be too violent, please go directly to Chapter 16.

Sincerely,
The Storyteller Guy.

Chapter 15
Evan and Bump Escape (The R-rated version)

"GO ON, BUTT-VHUT!" the Tall Dane said with a big dumb grin on his face. He was holding the great Golden Uni-corn in one hand and a plain old ear of corn in the other. "YOU TAKE ZA UNI-CORN AND I PROMISE I VILL NOT VACK YOU WITH ZIS *OTHER* PIECE OF CORN, YA?!"

Evan reached out and took the uni-corn.

Whap!

"OWCH!" Evan cried, putting a hand to his forehead, the very spot where the Dane just whapped him. "What did you hit me for?! You just said you wouldn't!"

"BECUZ YOU SHTOLE ZA UNI-CORN!" the Tall Dane said. "YA!"

Whap! Whap!

"OWCH! OWCH!" Evan cried, trying to shield himself from the attack. "I did not shteal your shtupid uni-corn!" Evan was having a hard time shaking the Danes infectious accent. "I mean I didn't *steal* your stupid uni-corn! You just gave it to me two seconds ago, you...you...you happy Danish person!"

"I KNOW ZAT! BUT EET'S MUCH MORE FUN TO SAY ZAT YOU SHTOLE EET," said the leader of the Danes, dancing and chasing Evan around the fire. "ZAT VAY, I CAN VACK YOU WITH ZIS *OTHER* PIECE OF CORN!"

Whap! Whap! Whap! Whap!

"THIEF!" the Tall Dane yelled. "THIEF! HE SHTOLE ZA GREAT GOLDEN UNI-CORN!"

All the Danes rushed over to help, but they had to keep dancing so it took them a while. Thank goodness Evan was much quicker than the Dancing Danes. He was able to zig and zag, wiggle and squiggle his way through the crowd of riled up Scandinavians. But Evan and

Bump's luck had run out. They had to escape, and *qvikly*, because the Danes had suddenly turned angry. And they were closing in on them.

Evan and Bump tried to run every which way, but found no escape. There were too many Danes. Eventually, the two of them would be captured and forced to dance forever.

However, before things dragged on too long, Bump came up with an idea to save the day.

"I've got an idea!" Bump said. "STOP, DROP, AND ROLL!" And that's exactly what they did. First they stopped, then they dropped, and then they rolled away. That way, because the Danes weren't able to stop dancing due to uncontrollable happiness, no one—not even the Flexible Dane—was able to grab a hold of them.

"It's vurking!" Evan shouted. He and Bump were much too quick for the Danes. Bump had been rolling since he was a baby log, and Evan was a quick learner.

"Roll for your life!" Bump shouted.

"HEY, VAIT UNE SECOND!" the Tall Dane hollered, chasing after them with an angry mob of Danes right behind him. "YOU CAN'T LEAF NOW! VEE

JUZT SHTARTED ZA NEW SONG! BEZIDES ZAT—YOU SHTOLE ZA GREAT GOLDEN UNI-CORN!"

Evan and Bump didn't stop. They just kept on rolling with it!

"VEE VUR GOING TO MAKE YOU VERY HAPPY," said the Dane's leader. "BUT ZEN YOU HAD TO GO UND SHTEAL ZA GREAT GOLDEN UNI-CORN! NOW VEE ARE VERY ANGRY DANES AND CANNOT POZZIBLY VIN ZA HAPPIEST COUNTRY IN ZA VURLD CONTEST DIS YEAR! AND EET'S ALL YOUR VAULT! GET ZEM, UNHAPPY DANES!!!"

The Dancing Danes were sure mad that Evan took the Golden Uni-corn, even though he really didn't. Still, for being mad, they all looked pretty darn happy. This was probably because they continued to dance, and smile, and wave their Danish flags.

"This way, Evan!" Bump called to his friend. The two of them headed for the path that led back to the big red door.

"COME BACK, BUTT-VHUT!" shouted some anonymous Danish person. Their sudden angry vibe didn't matter because by the time the Danes got halfway down the path, they forgot why they were chasing Evan and Bump in the first place.

"YEZ, COME BACK!" called some other Dane. "VEE MISS YOU ALREADY! AND YOUR TALKING LOG FRIEND, TOO!"

As soon as they felt that they were far enough away, Evan and Bump stopped rolling. Somehow, incredibly, probably to save time, Evan and Bump quickly found their way back to the beginning of the Forest of Flatulence.

They were back at the big red door.

Butt vhut they didn't know was that a bunch of red jumpsuits with dancing people inside them were (*gasp!*) standing right behind them!!!

The Danes obviously knew a shortcut.

"HELLO, BUTT-VHUT!" the Tall Dane hollered from the crest of the hill. The Danes were barely twenty yards away. "VEE ARE ZORRY FOR ZAYING YOU SHTOLE ZA UNI-CORN, BUTT-VHUT! VON'T

YOU PLEEZ COME BACK? VEE VILL MAKE YOU AN HONORARY DANE! VEE VILL DANCE, AND ZING, AND BE *ZOOOO* HAPPY!"

The leader of the Danes tried to do some kind of crazy break-dancing move, but he toppled over and got his arms and legs all tangled up. "UH-OH! I VENT WHOOPSY! AND NOW I ROLL DOWN ZA HILL TOVARDS YOU!"

A huge pile-up of Danes was now tumbling down the hill towards Evan and Bump, collecting speed.

"Oh no! Vee can't open za door from dis side!" Evan shouted, still trying to shake the Danish accent. Pulling on the door was pointless since there wasn't a door knob on their side.

"Did you try knocking?!" Bump suggested.

"Vye didn't I think of zat!" Evan cried.

Evan pounded on the door as the Danes tumbled down the hill, headed straight for them. He and Bump were frightened, and terrified, and scared, and any other words you can think of that mean exactly the same thing.

The Danes were less than ten meters away! Or in other words, roughly thirty-two feet and eight inches away!

Ten meters...

Nine meters...

Eight meters...

Seven meters...

Six meters...

Etcetera...

Etcetera...

"Who is it?" asked a familiar voice on the other side of the door. It was Red the Boy-cycle, of course, since everyone had probably forgotten about him by now.

"It's me! Us! Whatever!" Evan cried. "Open the door, Red! *Hurry*!!"

Five meters...

Four meters...

Three meters...

Two meters...

Isn't this...

Exciting...!?!

"*Me?* Me who?" Red asked.

The Danes vur—*were*—just centimeters away, which, in case you were wondering, was calculated using the metric system because that's what the Danes use.

"It's Butt-Vhut!" Evan yelled. "I mean *Evan*. It's me, Evan! Open up! THE DANES ARE COMING! THE DANES ARE COMING!"

One meter...

Suddenly, even though he didn't have fingers or an opposable thumb, Red miraculously opened the big red door. Evan and Bump raced through the opening and slammed the door shut just in time. The door bulged quite a bit, but there was no huge THUMP! like one would expect from an entire settlement of Danish people slamming up against a door.

"That was close," Bump said.

"No kidding," Evan said, his heart still racing. "A little *too* close."

Looking around, Evan saw that it was daylight once again. Inside the Forest of Flatulence it had been dark, but conveniently it was daytime once again. Evan shook his head at the convenientness of it all.

Red was stirring with excitement. "Excuse me, sir? Madam? Whichever the case may be?" Red drove in circles all around Bump, his eyes wide with curiosity. "Are you a talking log? Are you? Are you?!"

"Yes," Bump said, glaring at the excitable talking tricycle.

"Weird!" Red said, meaning no harm. He was just a little excited to meet a talking log.

"Oh? And I suppose being a talking tricycle is perfectly normal?" Bump was a little offended by the young boy-cycle's comment. "Who are you, anyway?"

"Sorry, I forgot," Evan said, apologizing for not making proper introductions like his parents taught him, giving the reader a valuable life lesson even though this wasn't supposed to be a book with cheesy reminders built in. "Red, meet Bump. Bump, meet Red."

"Hello, pleased to meet you."

"Hello, pleased to meet you too."

Now that everyone was introduced, and safe from the Danes, it was time to figure out what to do next. Evan was now unicorn-less, which meant he still had no way to get home. (*If it hasn't been mentioned already, Evan dropped the great golden ear of corn during their daring escape.*)

"So now what, huh? Now what?" Red asked, hyper as ever. *Brrring-Brrring! Brrring-Brrring!*

"Yes, Evan. What do you suppose we do now?" Bump asked. Even he was curious as to what happens next in the story.

"Well, I suppose we go on to the second quest," Evan said as he got on top of Red. "Hey, since we've come this far already, we might as well keep going with this ridiculous story, right guys?"

"Indubitably!" Bump said, whatever that meant.

"Woo-hoo!" Red said, which everyone could understand.

"To the Odiferous Underground!" Evan cheered, pointing to another wooden signpost that had magically appeared out of nowhere.

ODIFEROUS UNDERGROUND THIS WAY

Chapter 16
The Odiferous Underground

Without bothering to give much explanation, clarification, or even any description of their journey, Evan, Red and Bump made it safely to the Odiferous Underground. Now the three of them were looking down at a sewer grate which was inexplicably right in the middle of the dirt path.

"Wonderful," Evan said, staring down at the grate with his new friends. "I have to go down *there*?"

ENTER HERE

(One at a time, please!)

"Aw, man," Red said, looking sad. "This time I'm too big! I can't possibly fit down that round hole. Hey, I bet Bump can fit because he's round!"

"Uh, no. I, uh...I have sensitive nostrils," Bump said. "Looks like I can't go down there either. I guess you're on your own, Evan."

So just like the first quest, Evan had to go alone. With the help of his friends, neither of which had hands, the heavy grate was pulled up to reveal the black hole underneath.

"Wish me luck!" Evan said to his friends, as the second quest got underway. He began to climb down the ladder into what he assumed was going to be a stinky, smelly, rotten, disgusting, awful sewer.

"Good luck!" Bump hollered down to Evan.

"Smell ya later!" Red said. Then he and Bump started sliding the heavy lid back in place. "Don't want anyone falling in!"

Before Evan could ask, "How are you guys able to move that heavy grate if neither one of you has arms?!" the sewer grate was put back in place. This left Evan in pitch black, super-blackity, black darkness.

"Only scared little babies are afraid of the dark," Evan told himself, continuing to climb down. "Yeah, only little kids are afraid of the dark. So that means I stopped being a scared little kid ages ago."

Down...

Down...

...Down.

After an undetermined amount of time, Evan made it to the bottom of the sewer. Fortunately, the place didn't smell all that bad, considering it was a sewer. But it certainly didn't smell all that *good*, either.

Evan fumbled around in the dark, still pretending to *not* be scared. He had to tell himself over and over that he wasn't afraid of the dark.

"Nope, I'm not scared one tiny bit at the moment," Evan said, trying to act all macho. "What's the worst thing that could happen to me down here, in the dark, all alone?

Even if I *did* hear some terrible growling noise coming from a terrifying monster with razor-sharp teeth, all I have to do is climb back up the…"

Evan patted the wall.

"I *said* all I have to do is climb back up the…"

As Evan was having yet another conversation with himself, his hand was busy searching the wall for the ladder he just climbed down. The only problem was that the ladder wasn't there anymore. To make things excruciatingly clear: the ladder was gone.

"Hello?" Evan said. "Anyone home?"

Suddenly there was a terrible growling noise which may or may not have come from a terrifying monster with razor-sharp teeth. It could've just been Evan's imagination. Or perhaps it was his tummy rumbling?

"Rrrrrrrrr—"

Either way, *now* Evan started to panic. *Now* Evan started to be scared. *Now* Evan started to act like a frightened little kid, even though ten seconds ago he said he was well past that stage of his life.

Evan searched and searched for the ladder, but he couldn't find any trace of it. He did manage to find something else: a light switch.

Yes, there was an electrical light switch coming right out of the wall, which was made of dirt. And everyone knows that electricity doesn't come from dirt. Wisely, Evan didn't spend too much time thinking about how ridiculous this was, and neither should anyone else.

"Eureka!" Evan said, as if he was some kind of outdated scientist. He flipped the switch on. And just like in most cases, light suddenly filled the room.

"Hey, wait a second—" The room Evan was standing in wasn't a gross sewer after all. In fact, the room looked very familiar. Somehow, inexplicably, he found himself inside his father's workshop, which was really just the garage.

Everything was exactly the same as it was back home. The old lawnmower was in the corner. The old coffee can with all the nails in it was sitting on the workbench. And father's wall-o-tools, with each tool in its properly chalk-outlined place was the same as it had always been.

There was no monster.

But there *was* a tunnel.

Past the garage, where there *should* have been the door leading back to the kitchen, there was a tunnel. A huge tunnel that was big enough for a very tall person to walk through without bumping his (or her) head (or heads).

"Or a very tall *monster*," Evan accidently said out loud, accidently scaring himself. Looking around the room, he realized that following the dark spooky tunnel was the only way he *could* go.

"No problem," Evan said, ignoring his labored breathing and accelerated heart rate. "I'll just take this flashlight—" He took the flashlight from the workbench. "And this rubber mallet." He grabbed the rubber mallet down off the wall-o-tools. He figured that a hacksaw would probably be a better weapon to use against a dangerous monster, but father *never* allowed him to use any sharp tools without adult supervision.

"And neither should you, kids!" Evan told the audience, suddenly turning into some kind of Safety Advisor Guy against his will.

Thankfully, Evan quickly dropped the Safety Guy act and began to creep through the dark tunnel.

Chapter 17
The Odiferous Underground (Continued)

The tunnel kept going down at an angle. With each step Evan took, he was getting further and further away from civilization, and closer and closer to severe grossness.

"Yuck!" Evan said. "Smells like dirty socks down here. Dirty socks stuffed with rotten eggs. My *dad's* stinky socks."

After an undetermined amount of time, Evan began to get nervous that he might never find his way out.

Then he saw his first sign, which did absolutely nothing to calm his fear.

TERRIFYING MONSTER
THIS WAY

Then came this sign:

I'M *NOT* KIDDING!

Then this one:

TERRIFYING MONSTER
ANY MINUTE NOW!

And then this one:

OKAY, OKAY—

THERE IS NO TERRIFYING MONSTER.
BUT THERE *IS* A LOT OF SERIOUS
SCIENTIFIC WORK GOING ON HERE.

And finally this one:

TURN AROUND!
GO BACK!!!
(Pretty please?)

Evan finally made it to the main sewer system. He was now travelling along a cement walkway. The surrounding walls were made of bricks, not dirt. There were lots of fluorescent lights above, and also painted footsteps to use as a guide. To his immediate right was a foul river of much yucky stuff, whooshing along thousands of gallons of grossness.

"Ew, gross!" Evan said out loud for the sole purpose of letting everyone know just how bad it smelled. The smell was so awful that Evan was forced to pull his shirt up over his nose.

"What *is* this awful place?" Evan asked, venturing further down the corridor. He was in some kind of underground laboratory. Then he came across two more signs.

The second to last sign read as follows:

RALPH-TRONICS
LABORATORIES INC.

The last sign read:

QUIET, PLEASE!
CANINE GENIUS AT WORK!

And then, from behind the lab door, there came a terrible growling noise.

Chapter 18
Professor Ralph Barfolomule

"Grrrrrrrr…" came the terrible growling noise again. Then a male voice said, "At this rate it's never going to work. The timing is all wrong. And the electrical output of the magnaflux condenser unit is utterly useless. I simply cannot work under these conditions."

Evan stood in front of a lab door.

Professor R. Barfolomule
BHS, BPH, CCH, CLT, DDR, DrPH, DVM, ND, PhD, SC, SLS, SSV, VT.

Evan was about to put his ear up to the door to eavesdrop (*which, by the way, is very rude*), but the door suddenly swung open and a very irritated dog stepped out. Only *this* dog looked more like a scientist.

The scientist dog had big puppy dog eyes, floppy ears, and all the other usual cute puppy stuff. He also wore glasses, a pocket protector, a circular mirror on his forehead just like doctors used to do, and also one of those things that doctors use to listen to your heartbeat. He also wore a long white lab coat and walked on two legs just like a normal person.

"And who might you be?" the dog asked, peering down at Evan over his glasses. He shut the lab door before Evan could get a good look inside. "And what, precisely, are you doing in my laboratory?"

"Um, hi," Evan said, hiding the flashlight and rubber mallet behind his back. "My name is Evan."

"That answers my first question," the talking dog-professor said. "What about my second, third, and forth questions? The second question, need I remind you, was 'What are you doing in my laboratory?' And the *third* question was going to be how did you get down here into my laboratory? And fourthly, I was going to ask why you are hiding a flashlight and rubber mallet behind your back?"

"Well, my name is Evan…"

"Said that already."

"And I kind of *walked* down here," Evan told him. "So I guess that answers your second *and* third question. The flashlight was so I could see in the dark. The rubber mallet was in case, um…in case you were a terrifying monster with razor-sharp teeth that eats children for lunch."

"Hmmm…" The scientist dog had to think this over. He pulled a calculator from his coat pocket and began to punch in some numbers.

Evan had to wait.

"Well, as far as my calculations go, you can plainly see that I am *not* a terrifying monster with razor-sharp teeth that eats small children for lunch. What I *am*, though, is extremely busy. Now, if you'll excuse me, please do an about-face and go back the way you came. I need to get back to my experiments."

"Are you a scientist or something?" Evan asked.

"If you must know, I am a Molecular-eco-analytical-bio-chemical-environmental-toxicologist," the dog said.

"I am trying to discover a way of turning waste products into a useable source of energy."

"Oh. I've heard of a Zoologist, but never a Poo-ologist."

"My name is Professor Ralph Barfolomule, otherwise known as Ralph the—" Ralph stopped talking mid-sentence because he remembered something important. He pulled a small notepad from his coat pocket. "Ah, yes, I almost forgot. I am supposed to *sing* this part."

Then Ralph began to sing.

Well, hello! How are you?
I'm Doctor Ralph Barfolomule
Graduate of Harvard
An Ivy League School!

I'm a genius, a doctor,
A connoisseur of egg nog,
Known otherwise, and otherwise known
As Ralph the Barfing Dog

If you toot, how rude!
Quite disgusting, after all
But up-chucking, I say
Is completely nat-u-ral

What's causing this, you say?
I will find a cure, no doubt
In the meantime, I keep barfing
So the upstairs world kicked me out

Is he sick? Is he ill?

Does he have some strange disease?

No, of course not!

It's a case of the old dry-heaves!

The answer is NO

So please don't ask

If I beg, or sit, or enjoy doggie-treats

Of course not—

I'm a pedigree

I prefer Shakespeare, Moyer, and Keats

Evan liked this song a little bit better than the others, but not by much. "Ralph the Barfing Dog?" Evan asked with a suspicious look. "Why do they call you that?"

As if giving him a perfectly timed demonstration, Ralph put his hands on his knees—or rather, his *paws* on his knees—and began to dry heave.

"Hyuk...hyuk...hyuk..." Ralph convulsed violently for a while. Then he stood up straight and said, "False alarm!"

"Oh, I see," Evan said. "*That's* why they call you Ralph the Barfing Dog. Are you sick? Or do you always up-chuck when you meet new people?"

"Your second guess is correct, young man," Ralph said. "Meeting new people always makes me a teensy bit nervous, and then I get sick. That is precisely why I was kicked out of the upstairs world, as I clearly stated in my introduction song. I prefer my lab work to any type of interaction. This, of course, is why I put in my transfer to the Underground Experimental Research Lab." Ralph pointed to another sign, which Evan had somehow overlooked, or it had simply appeared out of nowhere. Either way, it read as follows:

Underground Experimental Research Lab

Nose protection <u>highly</u> recommended

Enjoy your stay!

"Nice to meet you, Ralph," Evan said, sticking out his hand. "I'm Evan Jacob Jacobson, visitor to your strange world."

Ralph and Evan shook hands. Paws. Whatever.

"Well, now that introductions are over with," Ralph said, "it is time to say goodbye. Goodbye!" And with that, Ralph the Barfing Dog spun Evan around and began to shoo him down the tunnel, back out the very same way he came.

"Wait!" Evan cried, digging his heels in. "You can't do this! I'm on a mission! I have a very important quest to complete!"

Ralph suddenly stopped shooing the young intruder down the tunnel. "A quest, you say?"

"Yes! I'm on a quest," Evan told him. "I came from another world that I'm trying to get back to. It's all because I broke my mother's favorite crystal unicorn figurine. When I tried to glue it back together, the Washing Machine Monster chased me. Then I found this hole in the wall. I went through it and met a troll, a log, and a talking tricycle. Then I met this short fat king guy—King Flibberti-something. He's the one who told me about the Three Quests. Now I have to find a unicorn to get home. And also because someone called Queen Mother will be mad and destroy everything if I don't find one." Evan was out of breath by the time he finished explaining all this.

"Another world, you say?" Ralph said, thinking it over. "Hmmm…" He pulled out his calculator once more and punched in a few numbers. "What was it that you said you had to find?"

"A unicorn."

Ralph's face suddenly turned sour. He pushed his glasses back up his snout and straightened himself up. Then, rather snobbishly, he said, "Oh. *Him.*"

"Him? Him who?" Evan wondered why Ralph suddenly got a very smug look on his loveable puppy dog face as soon as he mentioned the word unicorn.

"He's at the end of the tunnel," Ralph said, pointing down the hall. "Last door on the left. The room with the sound of utter laziness coming from inside. If you can get more than three words out of him, please ask him whether he will be leaving anytime soon."

Ralph the Barfing Dog went back into his laboratory, leaving Evan to walk down the tunnel by himself, past a bunch more doors, and past a bunch more signs.

NO SWIMMING!

NO BARKING!

NO VISITORS!

LAZINESS IN PROGRESS!

Evan stopped in front of the last door. He put his ear up to the door to listen, which back in Evan's world is called eaves-dropping, and is *still* considered to be very rude, the same as when it was mentioned a few pages ago.

Evan could hear the distinct sound of a television. Someone was watching a game show really loud.

Evan knocked.

"Come in!" said a kid's voice from the other side. "Close the door behind you."

Evan opened the door and was greeted by a very strange sight. A kid, probably about fourteen years old, was slumped on a couch, practically sinking into it. He was munching potato chips and staring mindlessly at a large screen TV. He had his feet up on the coffee table—another big no-no back in Evan's world. The kid looked bummed out, depressed, and thoroughly bored.

When Evan got closer, he could hardly believe his eyes. This frumpy, frowning, cynical-looking kid looked just like... *him*.

The kid on the couch was older Evan.

Chapter 19
Older Evan

Evan stepped inside the familiar room.

"Oh, it's *you*," said the kid on the couch. "Are you coming in, or what? Shut the door! Were you born in a barn?"

"No. A hospital," Evan told the kid. He stepped inside and shut the door behind him. Then he waited in silence for the older kid who looked just like him to say something. The lazy slug just kept staring at the TV like he was in some kind of trance.

"All these shows are so stupid," the older kid who looked like Evan finally said. "They're all so dumb."

"So why do you watch them?" Evan asked, inching closer, then very gently sitting down on the edge of the couch. Eventually, he worked up the courage to plunk down beside himself.

There was still no answer to his question. Older Evan just stared, and stared, and stared at the screen like a zombie.

"So…?" Evan said some time later. He wasn't sure how much later, but he was pretty sure it was after the first game show had ended and another one had begun. The older version of himself just kept on watching TV and saying absolutely nothing. "Never mind, I guess."

Evan wasn't quite sure where to start. Every time he looked at the kid on the couch, he felt like all the energy was being drained from his body.

Finally, Evan got up the courage to ask the kid his name. Naturally, Evan assumed the kid's name would be *Evan*. He assumed erroneously, which is just a really big word that means incorrect.

"What's your name?" Evan asked a second time, since the first time all he got for a reply was a grunt. He tried waving his hand in front of his older self's face. That didn't work either.

They both stared at the TV

(Hours and hours of TV later…)

"Yünni," the kid finally said. "My name is Yünni. Now can you *please* stop asking me all these dumb questions? I'm trying to watch the show."

"Ha!" Evan cried. "Your last name doesn't happen to be *Corn*, does it?"

"Yeah," Yünni said, flicking channels. "So what?"

"What?! Your name is *Yünni Corn?*" Evan asked, totally taken by surprise, just like everyone else who's following this story whether they admit it or not.

"No, genius," Yünni said. "What kind of dummy would have a name like *that?* My last name is spelled K—h—ø—r—n."

"I knew it!" Evan said, kicking his feet up on the coffee table. "I knew something weird was going on. Why else would this scene be happening?!"

They watched TV for a while.

"Look, Yünni," Evan said, as he reached for the bowl of potato chips. "I think you're supposed to go with me somewhere. At some point during this ridiculous adventure we have to meet someone called Queen Mother. Should we go now? Or maybe wait until the show is over?"

"*Go?*" Yünni said, giving Evan a dirty look. "Listen, dweeb. I don't *go* anywhere, okay? I just sit here."

"Yeah, I noticed," Evan said. "But you're a unicorn! Well, sort of, I guess. Your name is Yünni Khørn. That can't just be some kind of clever coincidence on that Storyteller Guy's part. I talked to that guy back in chapter three. Trust me, he's not that clever."

Yünni ignored him. He just kept on flicking channels, constantly complaining that there was nothing to watch. The TV they were both staring at was practically as big as the Jacobson's living room window. It probably had five hundred different channels to choose from, but the gangly, sour-faced kid with the lame peach-fuzz moustache still complained relentlessly.

"Um, please?" Evan tried to persuade his older-self to get his lazy bottom-side off the couch. "You have to come with me, Yünni. I need to go home!"

"What do you mean *go home?*" Yünni said, turning the volume way, way up. "You *are* home."

This is when Evan finally realized where he was. He wasn't in some strange room, or some stranger's room, or some stranger's strange room.

He was inside his bedroom.

Evan had travelled to a new world, met all kinds of bizarre creatures, came all the way to an experimental underground laboratory, and somehow he ended up in his very own bedroom. The posters on the wall had changed, but that was about the only difference. His favorite cartoon characters had been replaced with what he assumed would be his future favorite rock-n-roll bands. But that was about all. Other than a few changes, it was still the same old room.

They watched TV a little while longer.

During the entire time they sat there together watching TV, which was a very long time, Yünni made one cynical comment after another. It seemed that Yünni had absolutely nothing good to say about anybody.

"Don't you ever say anything nice?" Evan finally asked. "I've been listening to you for hours! Not once have you said something that's *not* cynical."

"What are you talking about?" Yünni snapped. "I'm simply stating facts. Everything is stupid and pointless. So all I'm doing is pointing out the stupidness and pointlessness of it all. What's wrong with that? Don't you get it?"

"Not really."

"Oh, just be quiet and watch the movie," Yünni said with a huff. "It's the stupidest movie ever made."

"How many times have you watched it?"

Yünni shrugged. "I dunno. Couple dozen times, I guess..."

Yünni Khørn was the most cynical person Evan had *ever* met. It took a while, but Evan finally came to the realization that he did not particularly *like* this older version of himself. In fact, Evan couldn't stand his future personality. But it was too late. Evan had already begun to sink into the couch.

At some point, Yünni passed Evan the TV remote.

And that was the end of the adventure.

The End

INTERRUPTION:

The Storyteller Guy is sincerely sorry for this interruption, but thought it must be stated that you, the reader, probably grew bored at some point and decided to go watch TV.

However, if Mr. Yunni Khorn didn't drain all your energy, then by all means continue reading.

Double-however, I must warn you that from here on out things get pretty hairy for Evan, Red, Bump, and Ralph.

Triple-however, if this doesn't frighten you in the least, please turn to Chapter 20.

Or go watch TV.
It's your choice.

Sincerely,
The Storyteller Guy.

Chapter 20
Older Evan
(The non-televised version)

Evan wasn't sure how much time had passed since he sat down on the couch beside Yünni Khørn. For starters, they watched back-to-back episodes of some game show, re-runs of a some old 1990's sitcom, and then sat through an entire series of movies. At one point, Evan was able to drag himself away from the TV long enough for a quick bathroom break.

Flick!

"There's nothing on."

Flick!

"That show was so dumb."

Flick!

"This one's lame. I've watched it eleven times."

Flick!

"Boring."

Flick!

"Stupid."

Flick!

Suddenly, to break up the monotony, and to speed the story up a little bit, there came a loud capitalized knock on the door.

KNOCK! KNOCK! KNOCK!

It was Professor Ralph Barfolomule. "Evan!" Ralph hollered. "Time to go!"

By this point, Evan had forgotten all about Professor Ralph Barfolomule, known otherwise and otherwise known as Ralph the Barfing Dog.

"Ralph!" Evan cried, still wedged into the couch. "I'm stuck in here! I can't stop staring at the TV! HELP!" Evan was just glad to hear a voice other than Yünni's voice, which never stopped being cynical, or rude, or annoying, or all three simultaneously.

"Go away, barf-boy!" Yünni yelled, continuing to *flick! flick! flick!* channels with the remote control. "Go back to your stupid science experiments! We're busy!"

"I must insist you come out at once," Professor Ralph said, sounding a teensy bit nervous. He tried the door knob, but wasn't able to open it from his side. "The time is now just a few minutes before twelve o'clock, noon. It is almost time for the daily flushing!"

"Um, Yünni?" Evan asked, even though it took a tremendous amount of energy just to use his brain to formulate this simple question, and even more effort to ask it. "What's the daily flushing?"

"Huh? Oh. It's when all those creatures up top use the bathroom," Yünni explained. "Every day at noon, there's one big flush, and this whole place gets flooded for a while. It's pretty gross. But hey, don't blame me. I didn't write this story."

Flick!

"Hey, check this show out. You'll like it. I've seen it probably a hundred times."

As soon as the show started, the whole place started to shake. The entire underground laboratory was vibrating. All sorts of nondescript stuff started to fall off of irrelevant shelves. At first, Evan thought it was an earthquake. Only now did he realize why Ralph had sounded so worried four paragraphs ago, back when the daily flushing was first mentioned. Evan tried to ask Yünni if they should find a place to hide.

"Shhhhh!" Yünni hissed at him. "I'm trying to watch the show. Be quiet."

"Um, Yünni?" Evan could feel the tremors getting worse. "I think we need to go. Right now."

"Look, little man," Yünni said, snatching the remote back from Evan. "I already told you that I don't *go* anywhere." He brushed the crumbs off his shirt, then reached for the magical bowl of never-ending potato chips.

"Yeah, we've been through that already," Evan said, blinking his eyes back into focus. Although it took a while,

Evan came to the realization that if he didn't stop being such a cynical, know-it-all kid *right now…*

"Then I'll grow up to be just like Yünni," Evan said, finishing off the previous sentence with some introspective dialogue. And if that was the case, Evan's life would consist of nothing more than staring at the TV and making rude comments about everyone and everything.

[CRUCIAL MOMENT ALERT!!!]

Evan felt something welling up inside him. He was choosing to leave the cynical life behind.

Suddenly he began to yell at Yünni Khørn, calling him all sorts of bad names that are not appropriate for this book. Nothing *too* bad, just stuff like "lazy bum" and "know-it-all noodle brain" and "selfish snot doodler." Evan wasn't exactly sure what a snot-doodler was, but it sounded good at the time.

"I don't want to end up like you," Evan told his future self. "All you do is complain, complain, complain! You don't like *anything*. Nothing is good enough, cool enough, loud enough, quiet enough, big enough, small enough, near enough, far enough, crunchy enough, chocolaty enough, sweet enough, fun enough, exciting enough—"

Evan stopped.

"Wait a second—?" Evan suddenly got a strange look on his face when he realized that this last outburst sounded *exactly* like an earlier description of himself from way back on the first page.

Oh, yes! This was a great self-realizing moment for Evan Jacob Jacobson.

"No kidding, Storyteller Guy!" Evan shouted at the italicized voice that came out of nowhere. "I'm still *having* this great self-realizing moment, dummy! How about a little privacy?!"

"No problem," the Storyteller Guy said. *"Sorry for interrupting. I'll just let you get back to degrading your future self."*

"Gee, thanks," Evan said, using up his last bit of residual sarcasm. After the intrusive intrusion from the Storyteller Guy, it took Evan a moment to remember why he'd been so mad in the first place.

Then he remembered.

181

"And I'll tell you *another* thing," Evan said, quickly forgetting about the Storyteller Guy's interruption and going back to yelling at Yünni Khørn some more. But Evan didn't need to yell at his future self much longer.

Yünni Khørn was beginning to fade away.

First he was kind of fuzzy. Then he was kind of *more* fuzzy. Then more and more fuzzy, until he was *really* fuzzy. And just like that, suddenly, fast but not too fast, quick but not too quick, eventually, finally, after way too many descriptive words, *thankfully*...

Yünni Khørn was gone.

Evan had just vaporized his lazy, annoying, cynical future self. Yünni Khørn was nothing but a puff of smoke, leaving behind only two cheeky imprints on the couch.

"Excuse me, Evan!" Professor Ralph said from the other side of the door. "Have you finished vaporizing your lazy, annoying, cynical future self yet?"

"Yes! Now I'm a...I'M A MURDERER!" Evan cried, feeling guilty for destroying his future self, who was conveniently named Yünni Khørn strictly for the benefit of a constant theme.

"No, no, no," Ralph said, finally able to enter the room now that Yünni was gone. "You are not a murderer, Evan. You have merely destroyed a possible future representation of yourself. Yünni Khørn was not real—not yet. But he *could* have been real if you hadn't been so brave just now and gotten rid of him…something I am extremely grateful for."

Evan was almost in tears thinking about how he was probably going to be sent to jail for the rest of his life, *again*. Ralph helped the hero of the story to calm down by explaining to him that he had made the right decision.

"Geesh," Evan said, standing up on his feet and checking out the indentation his bottom-side had made on the sofa cushions. "Is that really what I was going to be like as a teenager?"

Ralph pulled out his calculator for the third and final time and punched in some numbers.

"Yes, indeed!" Ralph said. "In seven years, eight months and sixteen days, you would've been just like him."

GRRR-BLE! GRRR-BLE! GRRR-BLE!

A very loud and oddly-spelled noise suddenly came out of nowhere to remind Evan, Ralph, and everyone else that they were still in danger. The underground laboratory was *still* shaking terribly. Much more terribly than the first time it was mentioned a while back. It sounded like the walls were about to cave in at any second.

This meant that it was time for a daring escape!

The first thing Ralph did was run back to his laboratory. He came back a moment later with two bright yellow rain suits. One was an XL, the perfect size for a tall scientist dog, and one was a size Small, the perfect size for a *formerly* cynical young boy on a rollicking adventure.

"Ah, there we go," Ralph said. He pointed at a tiny blue boat that was shaped like a urinal cake, which, in case you're a girl and don't know what a urinal cake is, it is a rice cake shaped thing that is used in boy's bathrooms to keep them smelling fresh and minty.

The tiny blue boat that had conveniently appeared out of thin air was tied to one of those boat tying things, floating in the murky brown water. The murky brown water, Ralph explained, was named the River of Muchyuckystuff.

"For *obvious* reasons," Ralph said.

"Um, Ralph? We're not going to float down this nasty disgusting river in that tiny boat shaped like a urinal cake, are we?"

"Of course we are! This boat is made of an indestructible material which I invented years ago," Ralph said, looking very proud. "It's called Flubby-non-toxic-half-plastic-half-polyurethane-three-quarters-carbonated-epoxy-primer-resin-3000."

"I don't care what it's made of!" Evan shouted, hurting Ralph's feelings a little bit. "No way am I getting into that thing!" Evan decided that he was not getting into a tiny boat that looked like it might sink, and then float down a slimy, yucky, raunchy river of sewage. But as soon as he turned around and saw the rushing tidal wave of gloppy goop coming towards them, he quickly changed his mind.

"Let's boogie!" Evan said. Quickly, he put on his rain gear and got into the boat, and not a moment too soon.

"Right on time," Ralph said, gripping the side of the boat. "The noon flushing is on its way!"

"Aw, man! This is *gross*!" Evan was upset because a big splat of grossness landed on his rain suit. "How long is this grossness going to last?!"

Ralph had to shout to be heard over the noise. "It's hard to say, Evan! We are at the mercy of a severely perturbed imagination! How does that ridiculous saying go? The one about rolling?"

"You mean, just roll with it?'" Evan said.

To which Ralph replied, "That's the one!"

Chapter 21
The River of Muchyuckystuff

Evan and Ralph sailed down the River of Muchyuckystuff. The ride was quite disgusting and much too filthy to describe.

Hence the short chapter.

Chapter 22
Hello New Friends

Evan and Ralph made it safely out of the Odiferous Underground. Red and Bump were waiting for them topside. Evan made some hasty introductions, then off they went.

Chapter 23
Goodbye New Friends

It was now time for the third and final quest.

"Thank goodness!" everyone cheered.

Unfortunately, Evan, Red, Bump, and Ralph were all suffering from a feeling of lostness. And the reason for this feeling of lostness was because they were lost.

The dirt path which had led them to the Castle, the Forest of Flatulence, and the Odiferous Underground was not being very helpful right now.

With Evan riding on Red, Bump rolling along on one side, and Professor Ralph running along the other side, the four of them were experiencing repetitive *déjà vu*. The dirt path just kept repeating itself over and over, until they were all sick of seeing the same stuff. They kept passing the same hills, the same grass, the same huge oak tree off in the distance, the same *everything*. They passed the huge oak tree fifteen times before someone finally noticed the door.

"STOP!" Bump cried, getting tired of rolling over his face and getting nowhere. "There's a door! A door is—OWCH!—carved into that tree that we've passed fifteen times!"

Bump stopped rolling. Ralph stopped running. Red screeched to a halt, and Evan went flying over the handlebars, like always. Then Ralph pulled out his calculator, even though the last time he used it was *supposed* to be the last time, and punched in a few more numbers. Everybody had to wait.

"Uh-huh…uh-huh," Ralph mumbled. And with some figures figured out, some coordinates coordinated, he was able to precisely locate their precise location.

"Well?" everyone asked.

"According to my calculations," Ralph said, "we are precisely where we ought to be." He pointed a paw toward the small door carved into the tree. A door, by the way, that looked *exactly* like the door to Evan's tree house back home. The same tree house that his father built for him two years ago, and that he hardly used anymore.

Once again, Evan had to go it alone. There was no sign that stated this fact, but the other two quests were solo jobs, so it only goes to reason that this one should be too.

"Well, here we are," Evan said. "The final quest. I wonder if things will be normal from here on out?"

Nobody seemed hopeful about that.

"Well, the sooner I get this last quest over with," Evan said, "the sooner I can get home." He was just about to knock on the door when he turned to look back at his friends. This was the third and final quest, so Evan had no idea if he would ever see them all again? The four of them had been through a lot together.

It was tough to say goodbye.

Having a talking bike, a talking log, and a talking dog for friends was pretty weird, but Evan didn't care. They were different, sure, but they'd always been there whenever he needed assistance, or help, or guidance, or any other word that means the same thing. They were the best friends Evan had ever had.

"Good luck, Evan!" Red said.

"Hope you don't get eaten alive," Bump said.

"Cheerio!" Ralph said, momentarily sounding like some proper English chap.

"Will I ever see you guys again?" Evan asked with a sad look on his face.

"Oh, I'm sure we'll pop up out of sheer convenience at some point!" Professor Ralph said.

It was a very sad moment.

Please take a moment to be weepy if you need to.

(Ready to proceed??)

Chapter 24
The Sea of Wonk
(Pt. 1 of 10)

Knock! Knock! Knock!

Evan knocked on the door three times, just as stated above. The door opened and he stepped inside the tree house. Once inside, the door shut behind him and quickly molded back into the tree. There was no going back now. He was trapped.

Evan cautiously stepped through the foyer, down the hallway, then tiptoed into the kitchen. The tree house was just like a regular house, except that it was inside a hollowed out tree.

"Hello?" Evan said. "Anyone home?"

No answer.

"Guess I'll try the second floor," Evan said, fully aware

that he was talking to himself like people sometimes do when they're nervous.

Usually, in previous chapters, things happened pretty quickly. Lots of action, lots of silly creatures, and lots of things to do. But this quest, so far, was kind of boring. There were no people, no creatures, not much of anything. It was just a big old spooky tree house completely filled with emptiness, whatever that means.

"This place is spooky," Evan said, trying not to spook himself. "Spooky and weird. And kind of familiar?"

Up the stairs he went.

CREAK!

SQUEAK!

& OTHER ONOMATOPOEIAS!

Evan continued to climb up the stairs, using the handrail for safety like a good boy.

Suddenly, a terrible thought popped into his mind. It went like this: "What if *this* story is a rip-off of that *other* story? That story about the grizzly bears who try to eat that annoying little blond girl with pigtails?"

So far the story Evan was involved in hadn't been like any other story he'd ever read before. Still, he couldn't help but wonder if the Storyteller Guy suddenly got bored with *this* story, and decided to rip off that *other* story and let the hero get gobbled up by a bunch of hungry bears that were sick and tired of eating porridge.

"Nah," Evan said shrugging it off. "He needs me. Isn't that right, Storyteller Guy? Um…hello? Storyteller Guy?"

No answer.

Evan continued up the steps. He didn't get *really* nervous until he made it to the top and saw three bedrooms, with three beds made up, just like in that *other* story.

"Uh-oh." Evan could hardly swallow. "Please don't let me get eaten by a bear. Please don't let me get eaten by a bear. Please don't let me get eaten by a bear…"

Evan pushed open the first bedroom door.

Nothing.

Evan pushed open the second bedroom door.

Nothing.

Evan pushed open the third bedroom door.

Something.

Chapter 24
The Sea of Wonk
(Pt. 2 of 10)

There were no bears in the room, thank goodness. But there *was* a little girl with pigtails. She appeared to be around five years old, wearing a checkered gingham dress with bric-a-brac trim.

"Who are you?" asked the little girl with pigtails. Her arms were crossed and she glared at Evan with two intense eyes—intense *green* eyes, the same color as Mother's eyes, which were also the same color as *his* eyes.

"Well? I'm waiting?" the girl said with a very snooty look on her face. But that's not the worst part. The worst part was that she and Evan looked alike—a *lot* alike.

"Who am I?" Evan asked, shutting the bedroom door and watching it mold into the house, just like the front door. Now he was trapped inside this rude little girl's pink, frilly, phoofy bedroom. "Who are *you*?!"

"I asked you first, doo-doo head," the little girl said as she seated herself on a plastic chair. In front of her was a plastic table, elegantly made up with plastic dishware. She'd been getting ready for a tea party when she was rudely interrupted. When Evan just stood there, refusing to answer her question, the little girl who looked just like him said, "You're such a baby."

"Am not."

"Are too."

"Am not!"

"Are too!"

"AM NOT!"

"ARE TOO!"

"AM NOOOOOOOOOOOOOOOOOOOOOOOT!"

"ARE TOOOOOOOOOOOOOOOOOOOOOO!"

"ENOUGH!!!" Evan shouted, finally giving up. "My name is Evan, okay?"

"Nice to meet you, Evan," the little girl said, changing from a yelling spazzball to perfectly calm just like that. "My name is Elinore Enid Jacobson. This is my room. This is my tea party. You may join me if you'd like. But only if you can *behave* yourself."

"Jacobson?" Evan's eyebrows rose up to the middle of his forehead. He was quite shocked when he realized how much this little girl really did look just like him, except more girly. But he was even *more* quite shocked when he found out they shared the same last name.

Evan sat down on one of the tiny plastic chairs and stared at her. Not in a rude way, just curious. After studying her for a moment, he was certain they had to be related. The resemblance was amazing.

"So, um, why do you look like me?" Evan asked, staring at her nose, which looked like his nose. And her hair, which was brown just like his hair. And her ears, which were kind of small and sticking out just like his ears. And her thoughtful, serious expression, which was just like his thoughtful, serious expression.

Elinore ignored him. She continued to pour invisible tea and dish out invisible cookies and biscuits. She just sat there and acted like some kind of proper tea-drinking, cookie-munching, biscuit-eating lady.

"I don't look like you," Elinore said, handing Evan a fake treat. "You're ugly. Besides, *you* look like *me.*"

"Do not."

"Do too."

"Do not!"

"Do too!"

"Do not!"

"DO TOO!"

"DO NOOOOOOOOOOOOOOOOOOOOOOOT!"

"DO TOOOOOOOOOOOOOOOOOOOOOOOO!"

"ENOUGH!!!" Evan yelled, cupping his hands over his ears. He couldn't believe what a brat this little girl who resembled him was. She was as much of a brat as Evan was when *he* was five years old, back before he discovered that being a *cynical* brat was much more sophisticated.

Evan knew he was fighting a losing battle. He may only be a kid, but he was wise enough to know that girls usually win contests and stuff just because they're girls, which means they're smart and clever, much more smarter and cleverer than boys.

"Hey, the Storyteller Guy is a perfect example of that!" Evan said, hurting the Storyteller Guy's feelings just a little bit. "And that's why good boys don't argue, or fight, or say mean things to girls!" Evan said, unwillingly turning into some kind of cheesy school counselor.

"Haven't you figured it out yet, silly?" Elinore said, helping herself to another invisible cookie. "I'm your *sister*."

"Huh?! Say what?!" Now Evan was *really* confused. Just a few minutes ago he was talking to a grumpy, cynical, bitter version of his older self. Now he was talking to someone who claimed to be his sister. Back home, in *real* life, Evan didn't have a sister.

"But I don't have a sister," Evan said, munching an invisible biscuit. "Not in real life."

"Not yet," Elinore said, using a real napkin to dabble fake cookie crumbs from the corners of her mouth. "But you will by the time this story ends! Have a cranberry scone, doo-doo head. I baked them myself."

"I don't want a scone," Evan said firmly, but politely, not wanting to start another screaming match. "I want to finish my last quest so I can go home, *doo-doo head*."

"Okay, fine," Elinore said. "Have it your way."

Evan stared at Elinore with his arms crossed.

Elinore stared back with her arms crossed.

Evan made a funny face.

Elinore made the same funny face—only better.

Evan frowned.

Elinore smiled a funny little smile.

"Why are you smiling at me like that?" Evan demanded. "That's a smirky smile if I've ever seen one."

"Haven't you noticed, silly?" Elinore pointed at the table. "I set out *three* cups for tea, and *three* plates for snacks. You haven't met my other tea party guest."

"And who might—" Evan began to ask, but a hyphen came out of nowhere and blocked his sentence. Out of the corner of his eye, he saw something big and green off in the distance. Whatever it was, it was coming towards them at a terrific speed. He stuck his nose up to Elinore's bedroom window, peering outside with his mouth hanging open. Soon his eyes were as big and round as something that's really big and round.

"What is *that*?" Evan asked, his body already trembling at what he saw outside.

At this very moment, a ninety-foot-tall broccoli-person was running towards them at full speed.

"Evan? Meet Brock," Elinore said.

Suddenly, there was a terrible crash.

CRASH!

And then a terrible roar.

ROOOOOOOOOOOOOOOARRRRR!

And then Evan was introduced to Brock.

Chapter 24
The Sea of Wonk
(Pt. 3 of 10)

"Good morning, Brock!" Elinore said, waving and smiling at the horrible green broccoli-monster that just smashed its humongous broccoli-hand through her bedroom window.

Elinore didn't even flinch. Evan, on the other hand, screamed his head off. And you would too if a real life broccoli-person the size of a *nine-story building* was reaching through a window to grab you.

"GOOD MORNING, ELINORE!" roared the giant broccoli creature. Then he picked Evan up, pulled him right out of the bedroom window and carried him off.

"Bye, Evan!" Elinore called from the broken bedroom window. "See you in a few months, doo-doo head!"

Chapter 24
The Sea of Wonk
(Pt. 4 of 10)

Evan was scared out of his mind. Seconds before, he was inside a nice quiet bedroom, eating invisible cookies and drinking invisible tea. Sure, he was stuck inside a pink, frilly, phoofy bedroom with a know-it-all girl who looked a lot like him, but at least he was safe.

Now he was being carried across fields of grass, wheat, milo, barley, and whatever else fields are made of by a nearly hundred-foot-tall walking, talking spear of broccoli.

"Where are you taking me, you big ugly broccoli person?!" Evan shouted.

"HOME," the giant broccoli-person said in his deep broccoli voice. "LATE FOR SUPPER. MUM SAID TO PICK OUT A NICE RIPE KID-MATO."

And before Evan could ask what a 'kid-mato' was...the whole world began to fade.

Evan fainted.

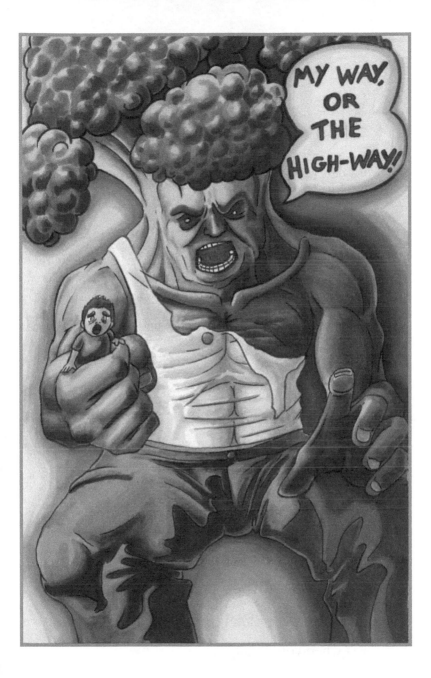

Chapter 24

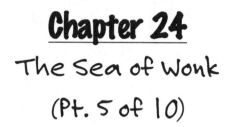

The Sea of Wonk
(Pt. 5 of 10)

Suppertime is usually a good time, especially if Mother prepares a nice meal with all your favorite foods. Or better yet, when your parents argue about money, but then decide that ordering pizza isn't *so* expensive.

There are also times when suppertime is not a good time. For example: when all the neighborhood kids are having a great game of hide-and-seek, or playing outside, then from the front porch, Mother yells, "EVAN JACOB JACOBSON! GET IN HERE FOR SUPPER OR I'LL SPANK YOUR LITTLE BOTTOM BLUE!"

That's when suppertime is kind of embarrassing.

But definitely, absolutely, positively the worst time for supper is when you *are* supper.

When Evan woke up after his fainting spell, he found himself lying on the world's biggest dinner plate. To Evan's right was the world's biggest scoop of mashed potatoes. To his left was the world's biggest heap of mixed veggies. Dead ahead was the world's biggest homemade biscuit.

"DINNER'S READY!" said another even larger broccoli person. "COME AND GET IT!"

When Evan had left the annoying little girl's tea party a few minutes ago, it had been bright and sunny outside. Now it was dinnertime. Wisely, Evan just shook it off, choosing to just roll with it.

Taking up their seats at the world's biggest dinner table were not one, not two, but *three* giant broccoli people. There was Brock, whom you've already met, plus two other green giants who were obviously Brock's parents. The Broccoli Mom had a big poofy green hairdo and wore an apron. The Broccoli Dad had a large green moustache and was reading the world's biggest newspaper.

"AW, MOM! KID-LOAF *AGAIN*?!" Brock whined, grimacing as his Broccoli Mom loaded up his gigantic plate with a huge slab. Brock immediately reached for the world's biggest bottle of ketchup, blobbing it all over the gross meatloaf—or 'kid-loaf' as the broccoli people called it. This was the only way Evan could eat meatloaf as well, with *tons* of ketchup.

Speaking of ketchup, Evan had to jump for cover as a huge blob of the delicious red condiment nearly splattered down on top of him.

"I *HATE* KID-LOAF," Brock said in a super huge, super whiny voice. "WHY CAN'T WE ORDER PIZZA?"

"TOO EXPENSIVE," Broccoli Dad said. "NOW BE QUIET AND EAT YOUR SUPPER!"

"STOP YOUR WHINING RIGHT NOW, YOUNG MAN," Brock's Mom said, speaking in capital letters just to show how gigantic she was. "OR ELSE IT'S OFF TO BED *WITHOUT* SUPPER!"

"LISTEN TO YOUR MOTHER," Broccoli Dad said, flipping through the newspaper, barely paying attention to the conversation.

Evan couldn't get his mind around the incredibly bizarre situation he found himself in. Just when he thought his adventure couldn't get any weirder, it did. Not just a little weirder. A *lot* weirder.

"Giant broccoli people?" Evan said to himself. "You've got to be *kidding* me?!!" Evan wished he could just faint again and go back to sleep. That way he wouldn't have to put up with any more of the Storyteller Guy's ridiculous plot twists.

"No!" Evan screamed when he saw Brock's fork aiming straight for him. "You can't eat me! I...I...I'll taste awful!" But his tiny voice wasn't enough to stop the world's biggest utensil from coming toward him. Luckily, Brock was such a spoiled brat that his Broccoli Mom had to cut his meat for him, which gave Evan time to run and hide. He hid behind the giant biscuit.

"AW, MOM!" Brock said. "CAN'T I JUST HAVE A PEANUT BUTTER AND KID-JELLY SANDWICH INSTEAD? *PLEEEEASE*?!"

Broccoli Dad neatly folded up his newspaper, then he slammed it to the table just like Evan's father did back home. He said, "QUIT YOUR WHINING, BUSTER, OR I'LL GIVE YOU SOMETHING TO WHINE ABOUT! NOW DIG IN!"

Evan spent the next few minutes running for cover every time Brock's giant fork came swooping down for another load. There were several close calls where he had to dive out of the way to avoid being scooped up. Evan finally realized that the only thing *not* being eaten were the veggies, which, in this backwards, crazy, messed-up world were called 'kiddies.'

"EAT YOUR KIDDIES," Broccoli Mom said, then gave Brock a vicious stare-down just like Evan's Mother did back home.

"AW, MOM! DO I HAVE TO EAT 'EM?" Brock whined. "KIDDIES TASTE *GROSS*."

"YOU WILL NOT LEAVE THIS TABLE UNTIL YOU'VE EATEN *ALL* YOUR KIDDIES," Broccoli Mom said. "EVERY LAST ONE! DO YOU HEAR ME, BUSTER?"

When Brock's dad finished eating, he belched. After saying, "EXCUSE ME," he snuck off to the den to watch the news. Brock's Mom began clearing the table, mumbling under her breath about how her loveable yet lazy husband always leaves her with the dirty dishes, kind of like how it happened back home.

"DON'T JUST PUSH YOUR KIDDIES AROUND THE PLATE, MISTER!" Brock's Mom yelled. "EAT THEM!"

"AW, MOM…"

(45 minutes later...)

Brock was still pushing his kiddies around his plate. Evan was completely out of breath from running. He dodged left, dodged right, and had to sprint from one end of the plate to the other to avoid being eaten. Finally, to speed up the story a bit, Brock came up with a tremendously brilliant idea. It was the same tremendously brilliant idea that Evan used every time *his* mother made him sit at the dinner table until he finished all his veggies: *The Milk Trick.*

To properly execute *The Milk Trick,* all you have to do is _not_ drink the very last gulp of your milk. Then you simply drop the peas—or whatever gross vegetable your mother is making you eat—into the glass. And then, just like magic—*poof!*—the nasty veggies disappear! It's a great trick, a classic, but it's always a good idea to wait until your mother's back is turned before attempting it. Also, you must be careful when you hand her your empty plate and your glass with one gulp of milk still in it. Because if she dumps it down the garbage disposal and *sees* the peas going down the drain, then there's really only one thing you can do: run for it.

Brock made his move.

The giant green teenager scooped Evan up into the world's biggest spoon, making sure his mom wasn't looking.

And then—

SPLOOSH!

Evan was drowning in wholesome 2%.

Chapter 24
The Sea of Wonk
(Pt. 6 of 10)

Finally, after an extended period of time, after suffering through five different parts of the same long chapter, Evan had finally arrived in the Sea of Wonk.

As you've probably guessed by now, the Sea of Wonk is actually a vast sea of milk. The word "wonk" may seem like a strange word to you, the reader, but it isn't to the Jacobson family. *Wonk* was Evan's first word.

One day, way back when Evan was a tiny baby, his mother and father were trying to teach him to speak. Father obviously wanted Evan's first word to be "Dad" or "Dada" or something like that. And Mother obviously wanted Evan's first word to be "Mom" or "Mama" or something similar. But Evan fooled them both.

"Can you say *Dada?*" Father asked.

"Wonk."

"Can you say *Mama?*" Mother asked.

"Wonk!"

"What did he say?" Evan's parents looked at each other with confused expressions.

"WONK!"

It took his parents a while to figure out what baby Evan was talking about. It eventually dawned on them when he stretched out his hands for the glass of milk his father was holding. Even though the proud parents were both disappointed that they didn't get their wish, they were still glad that Evan had learned his first word.

Not until first grade did they regret teaching him how to talk.

Chapter 24
The Sea of Wonk
(Pt. 7 of 10)

Evan was having trouble keeping his head above water. Milk. Whatever. His arms were getting tired, his clothes were beginning to weigh him down, and he kept taking huge gulps—mostly on purpose.

Evan was going under. He was about to become another victim of the mysterious Sea of Wonk.

"Help!" Evan cried. "I'm drowning in wholesome milk, which is high in calcium and Vitamin D!"

Chapter 24
The Sea of Wonk
(Pt. 8 of 10)

Suddenly, just so no one got *too* frightened, Evan saw someone else floating in the Sea of Wonk. There was still a chance for survival! At least he was pretty sure he saw someone else floating towards him across the milky white sea?

Oh sure, he could've been imagining it all, like a mirage. But Evan assumed that the Storyteller Guy was smart enough to know that a mirage happens in the desert, not the sea. Either he was going to drown in a sea of 2% milk or he would be perfectly okay, since you simply cannot let the hero of the story drown in the world's biggest glass of milk.

"Evan!" called a familiar voice. "You have to—OWCH!—keep dog-paddling!"

"Ex-*cuse* me, Mr. Grumpy-pants," said another familiar voice. "But I, being part of the canine family, find that term offensive."

"We're coming, Evan!" said a third familiar voice. "Hold on!" *Brrring! Brrring!*

Conveniently, floating towards him on the same tiny blue boat made of Flubby-non-toxic-half-plastic-half-polyurethane-three-quarters-carbonated-epoxy-primer-resin-3000, were his three friends, Red, Bump, and Ralph.

Evan was going to be saved.

If, and *only* if, his friends got there in time.

The next few moments were very worrisome.

(Pause here for added worrisome-ness.)

(continued)

"All right already! Enough of this ridiculous worrying!" Bump shouted at the beginning of the next page. "I can't stand it any longer! Evan's going to drown if we don't do something!"

Brrring! Brrring! Red agreed.

"Yo! Professor Dry-Heaves! Stop messing around with that stupid calculator of yours and toss me into the water!"

"Milk."

"Whatever!" Bump said. "Just pick me up and toss me! I'm surprisingly light!"

Evan was starting to sink. He accidently took a huge gulp of milk, then another, and then two *more* huge gulps. Then he laughed so hard that milk shot out of his nose. He was just about to go under when he felt his hand slip over some kind of round, buoyant, floating thing.

"Bump!" Evan cried. "You came to rescue me!"

"We all did!" Bump said. "Now let's get out of all this milk! It makes my skin all creamy and smooth, and I don't like that!"

Bump helped Evan stay afloat until the tiny blue boat pulled alongside them. It didn't take long because the urinal cake boat had some kind of high-performance motor. As the boat got closer, Evan could see that there wasn't a motor after all. It was Red.

Somehow, using all kinds of tie-downs and pulleys and other technical stuff, Professor Ralph had rigged Red to the back of the boat, and used his super-caffeinated energy to propel the boat faster than a speeding speed boat. And if you thought Red had the caffeine jitters *before*...boy-oh-boy, look out!!!

"Hi, Evan! Hi-Hi-Hi!" Red said as Ralph pulled Evan and Bump onboard. *Brrring! Brrring!* "When you left us in the last chapter, we all just sat around for a while. Uh-huh! Yeah, yeah! And then I snuck off—WOO-HOO! I snuck off and went back to The Town. You bet I did! I went back to that coffee place. You remember the one? That neat little cafe that sells yummy yummy coffee?"

"Yes, Red," Evan said. "I remember the—"

"YAHOOEY! I rode *aaaaall* the way back there before Bump and Ralph even noticed I was gone. You betcha! They've got a brand-new drink on the menu that's so delicious! It's called an octuple-shot espresso! Yeah, with cinnamon! I drank five of 'em!" *Brrring! Brrring!*

"It's great to see you guys!" Evan said, thankful for being pulled to safety, but also wishing for a cookie to go with all the milk he 'accidently' drank.

"Hello, Evan! It's good to see you, my boy!" Ralph said. "Didn't I tell you we'd appear out of sheer convenience?"

Evan gave each one of his friends a huge hug. It was awkward giving a hug to a log, a dog, and a hyper boy-cycle, but since Evan was still stuck in this bizarre story, he gave it his best shot. Mostly, he was just glad to be out of danger. Everyone took a moment to relax.

"Ahh," Evan said, now perfectly calm.

"Ahh," Bump said, now perfectly at ease.

"Ahh," Ralph said, doing some yoga.

Brrring! Brrring! "Yeah, yeah! I'm so relaxed I could—*Brrring! Brrring!* WOOT! WOOT! WOOT! *Cowabunga*!!"

Just when everything seemed okie-dokie…

Just when all seemed warm and squishy…

Just when a happy ending was moments away…

Just when you thought you couldn't stand one more "just when" sentence...

There was trouble.

Big, BIG, trouble.

"Uh-oh," Evan said, looking way, way down into the world's biggest kitchen sink. "Looks like big, BIG, trouble."

In case you'd forgotten, the four of them were all still inside the world's biggest glass of milk. How Evan got there we already know. But as for how the other three got there...that will have to remain a mysterious mystery.

And now the giant glass of unfinished milk was about to be dumped down the world's biggest garbage disposal. Tiny metal food grinding things were already tearing uneaten food to shreds. The mechanical monster was growling, shredding, and making terrible sounds.

GRRRRR—GRRRRRR—ARBAGE!

GRRRRR—GRRRRRR—DISPOSAL!

"HERE YOU GO, MOM," Brock said, handing over his glass of milk with the kiddies at the bottom. "MMMM, I LOVE KID-PEAS! THEY WERE DELICIOUS, MOM!" Brock smiled and rubbed his tummy. But he didn't want to overdo it, so he got out of the kitchen quickly, before he got busted.

"THAT'S A GOOD BOY," Brock's mom said, rinsing off his dish. "NOW IT'S TIME FOR YOU TO DO YOUR HOMEWORK."

"AW, MOM! DO I HAVE TO?" Brock was already lounging in the world's biggest den, where he was watching the world's biggest TV with his dad.

"GET UPSTAIRS RIGHT NOW, BUSTER!" Brock's Mom yelled. "DO AS I SAY!"

"LISTEN TO YOUR MOTHER," Brock's Dad said. He was watching broccoli-baseball on TV, hardly paying any attention to the conversation.

Brock's mom dumped out the last gulp of milk. Evan, Red, Bump, and Ralph were now falling through the air, just a few seconds away from being ripped to shreds by the world's biggest garbage disposal.

They were done for.

Goners.

Nothing could possibly save them.

No way.

No how.

Nothing in a rational, logical, sense-making world could possibly save them.

"Well, it's a good thing we're not in a rational, logical, sense-making world!" Evan said, hoping for a nice reassuring reply from the Storyteller Guy. "Isn't that right, Storyteller Guy? Hello?!"

Chapter 24
The Sea of Wonk
(Pt. 9 of 10)

"Noooooo!" Evan cried. He and his friends were mere nanoseconds away from the bitter end. "I'm too young to be garburated!"

"Wonderful," Bump said, grumpy even during his last few precious seconds. "I'm going to die while covered in milk. And I'm lactose intolerant!!"

"This does not compute!" Ralph cried, still managing to punch numbers into his calculator as he fell. "This does not compute!"

Brrring! Brrring! As for Red, he was too caffeinated to care that a giant garbage disposal was going to chew them up into little bits and send them all to their sludge-filled graves.

Chapter 24
The Sea of Wonk
(Pt. 10 of 10)

When it seemed that all hope was lost...

When it seemed that no one was going to help them, not even the Storyteller Guy...

When it seemed that the four main characters were about to be chewed up into bits...

A wonderful thing happened.

A real live *Unicorn* swooped down and rescued them all. And everyone lived happily ever after, for a very long time.

The End
(Again)

INTERRUPTION:

The Storyteller Guy is sincerely sorry for this final interruption, but thought it must be stated that you, the reader, should probably stop reading now. Things get extremely dangerous for Evan, Red, Bump, and Ralph from this point on.

However, if that ending did not satisfy you, and you are daring enough to read what <u>really</u> happened, then please go directly to Chapter 25.

But if your children—or you—wake in the middle of the night because of terrible nightmares after reading what really happened...don't blame me.

Sincerely,
The Storyteller Guy.

Chapter 25
On Trial

Evan, Red, Bump, and Ralph were on trial for their lives. All this happened right after the whole 'rescued by a not so smart unicorn' thing.

Chapter 26
The Whole 'Rescued by a Not So Smart Unicorn' Thing

The four of them got rescued all right. A real live unicorn really did swoop down and save them all from being chewed up into little bits by the world's biggest garbage disposal.

With the bitter end just seconds away, out of nowhere, out of nothingness, out of sheer luck, a great white horse with great white wings and a great white horn thing on its head swooped down and saved them.

It was a great rescue, to be sure. But what they don't tell you in stories is that real unicorns have a terrible sense of direction. Unicorns are beautiful and all, plus they have that really cool magical horn thing, but they're not highly-intelligent creatures.

"*Right!!*" Evan shouted, holding on for dear life as he and his three friends were flying in circles around the world's biggest kitchen. "Turn right! No, the *other* right!"

The unicorn made a sharp left turn, then went straight for a while. The creature's speed was amazing, but the unicorn sure didn't take directions well. Soon all of the passengers were getting nauseous—that is, except for the one passenger who was too hyper to notice how fast they were going.

"*Weeeeeeeeeee!* This is fun!" Red shouted, skipping over the explanation of how a boy-cycle without any arms or legs could possibly hold on to a unicorn.

"I get air sick very easily!" Bump said, also avoiding this same explanation.

The dumb white horse kept making left turns over and over like it was some kind of racehorse that couldn't break the habit. It took the four of them—*five*, including the left-turn-only unicorn—nearly twenty minutes to fly out of the giant Broccoli people's kitchen window. And just in time, too, because Broccoli Mom had just opened up the world's biggest kitchen drawer and pulled out the world's biggest fly swatter.

Luckily, they escaped.

It took them another half an hour to get a reasonably safe distance away. By that time, the *ooh*'s and *ahh*'s that such a wonderful mythical creature might normally get were quickly replaced with yelling, screaming, and unprintable swear words such as "manure head" and "chicken nugget brain."

"Turn right!!" Evan yelled the same thing again and again. "The *opposite* of left!"

Nothing worked.

"Neee-he-he-he-he!" the unicorn said, which made absolutely no sense to anyone. Incredibly, the one creature in this wacky world that *didn't* talk was the unicorn. All four passengers were shouting flight coordinates to a creature that couldn't understand a word they were saying. But that didn't stop them from trying.

"Whatever you do, Mr. Unicorn," Ralph said, leaning over Evan's shoulder to speak to the world's dumbest mythical creature. "Do *not* head for that little town just off in the distance, okay? That is the Castle. We certainly don't want to head over there, now *do* we, Mr. Unicorn?"

"Neee-he-he-he-he!" the unicorn replied.

"That is correct!" Ralph said, thinking he was actually getting through to the dumb animal. "*We* owe the king some back taxes. So *we* don't want to go there, right, Mr. Unicorn?"

Unfortunately, Ralph's reverse osmosis psychology didn't work. Guess what the dumb unicorn did? Take a *wild guess* where the unicorn headed?

You guessed it! The Castle.

Chapter 27
On Trial
(A more detailed look)

"THAT'S IT! KEEP COMING! JUST A LITTLE BIT FURTHER!" King Flibbertigibbet said in his extra loud voice with capital letters. The king held a megaphone in one hand, while using his conductor wand to guide the unicorn in for a landing.

"AND…*CUT*!!! CUT ALL ENGINES! WHOA, HORSEY!!"

As soon as they landed, Evan, Red, Bump, and Ralph were all arrested. The Seven Knights of the Week were standing off to the side, ready to slap the cuffs on. It was as if they'd known all along what was going to happen next in the story. King Flibbertigibbet came stomping over with his face all twisted up because he was the exact opposite of happy. He was yppah, which is a very difficult emotion to explain.

"Excellent job, Lefticious!" the king said, patting the great white horse's kneecap because that was as high as he could reach. "You've brought the criminals right to me! Such an unexpected surprise!" Then he gave the creature an all-knowing *wink-wink*.

"Neee-he-he-he-he!" Lefticious the Unicorn said, then walked off to get a drink of water.

"*Lefticious*?!" Evan said, looking skeptically at the king. "You've got to be kidding me?!"

"Don't blame me," King Flibbertigibbet said. "*I'm* not the one writing this ridiculous story. Slap the cuffs on! Hands *and* feet…if available."

The knights did as they were commanded.

"That's it, my good fellows!" the king said. "Slap the cuffs on! That's it, yes, good and tight!"

While having the cuffs slapped on, Evan was under the impression that King Flibbertigibbet was very fond of the expression *slap the cuffs on*, especially since he'd used it twice already.

"What's the meaning of this? This is absolutely preposterous!" Ralph said, using a really big word for no reason at all. He tried reaching for his calculator to see if this situation really *was* preposterous, but his hand was slapped away by Tuesday Knight.

"Questions will be answered *after* the executions," the king told him. "Go on, knights! Slap the c—"

"Don't say it," Evan said, cutting off the king before he could say his new favorite phrase again.

"Very well," King Flibbertigibbet said, lowering his head and looking sad. Then he quickly put the megaphone to his lips and shouted, "SLAP THE CUFFS ON!" Then he stuck his tongue out at Evan.

"Um, King Highness, sir?" Monday Knight asked. "We can't handcuff the boy-cycle or the talking log. They don't have arms or legs, your Royalness."

"Oh, very well then," King Flibbertigibbet said, already pulling his black judge's robe over his head. "Just tie them up with some of that braided fiber stuff we use to tie knots with."

"You mean rope?"

"Sure, that works too."

Then it was time to head off to the courthouse for an unfair trial.

So off they went!

Getting to the courthouse didn't take long at all, hence the immediate continuation of the story. The place was right there. And when I say *right there*, I mean just that. The courthouse was barely ten feet away.

"Well, that's convenient," Bump said. "Less distance to travel means less times I have to roll over my—OWCH—face."

"Irrefutably," Ralph said, using an uncommon big word that simply means "yep."

Everything was already set up, right there in the middle of Town Square, which was really shaped more like a circle. There was an entire courtroom in the middle of the street, complete with bleachers for all the spectators, a jury box, and two judge's chairs. One chair was kind of small, the perfect size for a height-challenged king. The other chair was much bigger and more important looking. If, let's say, Evan assumed that this bigger more important looking chair was for Queen

Mother, which he did, he would've assumed correctly, which he had.

The jury box was filled with Snippets, Whats, Aunts Golliwogs, and an assortment of other weird creatures you can conjure up with your own imagination.

The four prisoners were each placed on top of a wooden box. The angry mob of townsfolk was roped off, thank goodness, but they were still close enough to throw rotten vegetables and other gross stuff at the prisoners.

"GUILTY AS CHARGED!!" the jury shouted.

"Wait, wait, wait! Order in the court!" King Flibbertigibbet pounded his order in the court hammer. "You must wait for me to read the charges and *then* pronounce them guilty."

"Ahhh," the jury all said. "Gotcha."

"GUILTY AS CHARGED!" the crowd chanted.

"Hey! That's *our* job!" cried the jury.

The king stuck the megaphone up to his lips once more: "I HEREBY DECLARE THAT THESE FOUR TROUBLE-MAKERS—EVAN JACOB JACOBSON, RED THE BOY-CYCLE, BUMP THE GRUMP, AND PROFESSOR RALPH BARFOLOMULE—SHALL BE

PUT TO DEATH JUST AS SOON AS QUEEN
MOTHER SAYS SO!"

The creatures all cheered and ate cotton candy.

"Peanuts *hee-yuh*!" a vendor shouted, carrying all sorts
of goodies in his over-the-shoulder carrying bag. "Get
your fresh roasted peanuts *hee-yuh*! Popcorn! Licorice!
Bubble gum *hee-yuh*!"

The four prisoners all looked scared and/or nervous.
Just when things had started to look up in the last chapter,
they suddenly found themselves in the worst situation yet.

"What precisely are the charges?" Ralph demanded.

"Yeah, what did we do wrong?" Evan asked.

"This bites," Bump said.

"Yippeeee!" Red said, unable to sit still.

"Save all questions for after your execution, please!"
King Flibbertigibbet told them. The king was getting
upset by all the interruptions, but since his mood changed
so rapidly, he kindly explained the charges anyway.

The king said: "You four criminals are hereby charged
with unlicensed adventuring. Furthermore, so forth and
so on, you are guilty of rice cake thievery, rudeness to a
troll, interrupting a game of Knock 'Em Down, thieving

of my conductor wand, roasting marshmallows over an illegal campfire, endangering a Golden Uni-corn, unexcused sentence finishing, several hours of terrible dancing, being annoying while on trial, *and*, last but not least, plottingness to come back to this world whenever you want just so you can turn this ridiculous story into a series." When he was finished, the king took a bow and the whole crowd cheered.

After an undetermined amount of time, things finally settled down. The only thing left to do was to wait for Queen Mother to arrive so she could deliver the final judgment. So, while everyone awaited her arrival, King Flibbertigibbet entertained the crowd with lame magic tricks.

"Booooo!" the crowd shouted. "Boooooring!"

Suddenly, to keep things moving, Queen Mother arrived.

KA-SLAM!

The front door to the Castle ka-slammed open. A whole caravan of creatures carrying Queen Mother in a carriage came crashing in, cart-wheeling, caroling, and doing many other things that begin with the letter "c."

Queen Mother was a terrifying sight. She wasn't a Queen Mother at all. Well, she *was* a Queen Mother, but she was also a giant insect. More accurately, she was a Queen Bee. More accurately-er, she was a twelve-foot-tall *wasp* with a ginormously humongous stinger.

"Hail the Queen!" the townsfolk cheered.

Queen Mother was a rather attractive bee, as far as bees go, but she had a mean face. She wore lots of makeup, stylish clothes, and a large golden crown sat on top of her nicely-shaped head—which, by the way, was the complete opposite of King Flibbertigibbet's large, fat, round head.

"Hey?!" King Flibbertigibbet shouted in protest at the Storyteller Guy, who for some reason went way off topic. "I resent that! My large, fat, round head is the perfect size for my large, fat, round body, o-*kay*?!"

Also, if someone (*the Storyteller Guy*) forgot to mention it before, this certain someone (*the Storyteller Guy*) will go ahead and mention it now:

Evan is terrified of bees!!!

Chapter 28

The Bee Story
(In poem form)

Bees.

Big long stinger,

Playing in the woods

With my friends.

Allergic reaction

Mom said so.

Bit my hand

Bit my ear

Hurts a lot.

Swollen face.

Poem by Evan Jacob Jacobson & Mother

(6 yrs old, lying in bed with 27 bee stings)

Chapter 29

Queen Mother

(Introduction song begins on the next page.)

(Meanwhile...enjoy the only 'non-chapter' chapter of this book.)

I am Queen Mother

Quite unlike any other

I'm not your sister or your brother

I'm Queen Mother, you blundering blunderer!

My stinger is filled with poison

So don't make me angry

I love to sting little boys

And make them scream Ow-ee!

I'm the one in charge

Though I let the king believe

That he's the one in charge

But I'm really the Big Cheese

I don't care if dinner is late

Or if your ears are filled with wax

Oh, quit your sobbin'

It's not my problem

I just want to relax!

And I certainly don't mind

If my song doesn't rhyme

I'm Queen Mother, you stupid person

Now, rub my feet!

Make me a hot bath!

Fix me a cup of green tea! NOW!

Listen up, Buster—

LISTEN TO YOUR MOTHER!!!

254

Chapter 30
The Longest Chapter

Evan thought that Queen Mother's introduction song was just as bad as all the others, but also kind of scary.

"Well, don't just stand there admiring me, you fools," Queen Mother said with a dismissive wave of her bee hand. "Proceed!"

Evan immediately noticed that Queen Mother had some major attitude problems. But he didn't dare say this out loud.

Not yet.

Everyone stared at Queen Mother with a mixture of love and fear. When they didn't all snap to it, Queen Mother shrieked, "I told you to proceed with the proceedings!"

"Boy, she's got some major attitude problems," Evan said, forgetting to use his inside voice.

Brrring! Brrring! Red agreed.

The Queen's royal carriage was pulled right up to the judge's bench. Instead of walking two whole steps to her judge's chair, her group of slave creatures hoisted her up out of the carriage with some kind of hoisting mechanism, then gently placed her into her judge's chair.

"Geesh! Talk about lazy," Evan whispered, but not so quietly that the others around him couldn't overhear his rude comments.

Brrring! Brrring! Red agreed again.

"They should call her Queenie the Weenie!" Evan said, not quite sure what was wrong with him. He kept saying all these mean cynical things even though he already promised not to say mean cynical things anymore almost seventy pages ago.

Brrring! Brrring! "It's because this is the climax!" Red told him. "You know? The big exciting part at the end of a story?! This is when you have a great inner battle with yourself. Nobody will know until the very end how things turn out! Exciting, isn't it?!" *Brrring! Brrring!*

"Oh, I see," Evan said, troubled by this strange development. "Gotcha."

A hush fell over the crowd.

The townsfolk were completely silent. No one made a peep. No sounds at all. Not one little noise, *except* for all the whispering, gossiping, munching, lip-smacking, and chomping of all the goodies the crowd had purchased from the vendors.

Queen Mother raised her skinny bee arms while several creatures gently pulled her judge's robe over her head, doing so inexplicably without removing her crown or messing up her perfect beehive hairdo.

"Charges?" Queen Mother asked, as she checked her mascara in her little compact mirror. She was handed the court document by King Flibbertigibbet, who looked just as nervous as everyone else. Queen Mother barely glanced at the list of charges before adding even more charges.

Queen Mother announced very loudly: "Add to this list, mean cynical comments made toward me, your beautiful and precious Queen!"

The crowd gasped.

"The young boy who now sits on trial, Evan Jacob Jacobson, said the following words, which I will now quote: 'She has some serious attitude' and 'talk about lazy' to name just a few. Worst of all, he called *me*, your loving and nurturing Queen...he called me...*sniff-sniff*..." Queen Mother's bottom lip trembled as she whipped up some fake tears. She was really laying it on thick, trying to get everyone on her side.

"What did the little brute call you, your Queenliness?" shouted one of the townsfolk. Everyone glared at the boy who dared to insult their Queen Mother.

Queen Mother miraculously got a hold of herself. "He called me—" She stopped momentarily so she could read the updated document that was just handed to her. "He called me QUEENIE THE WEENIE!"

The Snippets yelled, "Nooo! Not *that*!"

Several of the Aunts fainted at hearing such atrocious atrocities.

The Whats said, "What?! What did she say?!"

All the other creatures began to shout and yell horrible things at him. Evan's friends all looked at him with a look of surprise, shock, amazement, and astonishment all rolled into one. It was quite an intense look.

"My goodness, Evan," Ralph said. "Those were some maliciously mean, ridiculously rude, and contentiously cynical comments you made about Queen Mother. I thought you decided to change your wayward ways? Remember? No more sarcasm? No more cynical talk?"

Evan shrugged. "Sorry, guys. I don't know what's wrong with me?! It's like all those *other* stories where the main character has a huge meltdown at the end, when nobody knows whether he's going to be able to battle through the intense emotions."

His friends all nodded sympathetically.

"And now, the protagonist—that's *me*, by the way," Evan clarified, "will probably have some tough decisions to make in the near future. This could mean putting the people he cares about most—that's *you guys*, by the way— in grave danger. It's all so heartbreaking, don't you think?"

Brrring! Brrring! "You bet it is!" Red said. "And the suspense is killer!!"

"But hey, you never know," Evan said, suddenly becoming optimistic. "Maybe, just maybe, everything will turn out fine in the end."

Evan's friends, the ones *not* so hopped up on caffeine that they couldn't think straight, weren't so sure. They were all extremely disappointed in Evan's cynical outburst. None of them knew what to tell him, so they all looked at their feet, or their bike pedals, or their crusty brown bark skin.

"Look, lady," Evan said, addressing Queen Mother in his old sarcastic tone. "I'm *really* sorry about those rude comments I made back at the beginning of the chapter. Honest, *Queenie*."

"Oooh!" taunted the crowd.

"Did you *hear* that sarcasm?" some random creature said. "He's in for it now!"

"Oh, be quiet!" Evan yelled at the crowd of annoying creatures. He was frustrated because he was no longer able to control his emotions.

"Okay, maybe I overstated a little bit by calling her Queen the Weenie," Evan told the crowd. "Hey, I'm a big boy. I can admit it. So she may not be a *weenie*, but she is definitely a *meanie*."

The crowd was absolutely stunned, and bamboozled, which is a much more fun word that means exactly the same thing.

"Well? It's true isn't it?" Evan was practically able to feel the tiny cynical organism-things coursing through his veins. "Just look at her sitting up there like some hotshot know-it-all Queen Bee. Who do you think you are, Queenie? I'll tell you who *I* am. I'm Evan Jacob Jacobson, visitor to your strange world. And since I got here it's been one crazy thing after another! I've had to deal with a grumpy troll, getting doors slammed in my face, getting lost in the woods, not to mention the fact that my bottom is sore from travelling all over this silly world of yours."

"Oh dear," one of the townsfolk said. "Nothing's worse than a sore bottom!"

"I agree!" hollered some other creature that was prone to sorebumitus.

The townsfolk were now beginning to side with Evan. Some of the female creatures were actually getting weepy as they listened to all of Evan's terrible sufferings. A few

261

of the creatures children were so horrified by the graphic details that they covered their eyes, not that this helped much with *listening*.

Evan wasn't finished. "I've had to put up with rude blue Mohawk creatures with intestinal problems, being hit on the head numerous times with a hunk of dried corn, then forced to dance for six and a half hours!"

Someone with a funny accent shouted, "EET'S TRUE! HE DEED ZA BOOGIE VOOGIE ALL NITE LONG! HE VIGGLED HIS LEETLE TUSHY AND EVERYZING!"

"I also had to put up with my lazy, annoying older self," Evan continued. "After that, I had to take a boat ride down a river of yucky stuff. I just about got eaten by a giant Broccoli-kid, then barely avoided being drowned in the world's biggest glass of milk. After that, I barely avoided being chewed up into little bits by the world's biggest garbage disposal. What's worse, I had to put up with a bratty little girl who claimed to be my future sister. And then…and *then*…" Evan was trying to think of other stuff to add. "Oh yeah! And *then* I came here and was put on trial for no reason at all."

The crowd applauded Evan's bravery. None of them had ever dared stand up to Queen Mother. They mostly just did whatever she said, whenever she said it, as fast as they possibly could. Things had been like this for as long as they could remember.

"The kid's right!" some creature shouted. "Queen Mother makes us do all sorts of stuff we don't want to!"

Another creature said, "Yeah! Even though it's usually for our own good and builds character!"

One group of nondescript creatures began to cheer, "E-van! E-van! E-van!" until the whole crowd was doing it.

Queen Mother rose to her full height to address the unruly crowd: "Creatures of the town! Please understand that I do all these awful things to you out of *love*. To teach you a lesson. To guide you. To discipline you. To help you make good decisions so you can grow up to be sensible, responsible people. Creatures. Whatever."

The crowd would not be persuaded.

"Surely, you must surely believe me?" Queen Mother said. "Not even a little surely?"

"But he finished the three quests!" an unimportant creature shouted. "Send him home!"

"Yeah! That was the whole bulk of the story!" another nameless creature hollered. "He did what you asked him to do. Now you're going back on your word!"

"Send him home!" the crowd cheered.

"SEND HIM HOME!"

"SEND HIM HOME!"

"ZEND HIM HOME, YA!"

"Oh yeah. Hey, they're right," Evan said, managing to stand up on his wooden box without any clear description of how this was possible with his hands *and* feet tied up.

"I forgot all about that part," Evan said, realizing this realization. "I *did* complete the three quests just like I was told by King Flibberty-what's-his-name."

"Flib-ber-ti-*gib-bet*!" King Flibbertigibbet shouted. "Is that so hard to say?!!"

"SILENCE!" Queen Mother demanded. "All of you!" She said this with such fierce ferocity that everyone, including Evan, stopped talking. This was followed by a very tense moment.

(Pause here for added tenseness.)

(continued)

"The king has lied to you, dear boy," Queen Mother said, crushing any hope Evan had of returning home. "As I clearly stated in my introduction song, he isn't really in charge. I am. I was the one who came up with idea of the three quests. I invented them for the last child who wandered into our world. That one, I'm afraid, disappeared some time ago. The last I heard, he discovered something called a TV."

"I can vouch for that!" Professor Ralph interrupted. "He's been living in my underground laboratory. Well, he *was* living in my laboratory... right up until Evan got rid of him."

"AHA!" King Flibbertigibbet cried, pointing a finger at Ralph. "I knew I knew you! You're that scientist dog who lives in that stinky underground laboratory. You haven't paid your taxes in eleven hundred years, you mangy mutt!"

Ralph tried to act all innocent. Then he started to dry-heave.

"Order!" Queen Mother shouted, bashing her hammer on the hammer bashing thing. "ORDER! I must have order!"

For convenience sake, order was soon restored.

"As I was saying," Queen Mother continued, "the three quests were invented as a way to distract you. To keep you occupied long enough so that you would forget all about going home. There really is no way back to your world. You weren't actually supposed to finish those silly quests."

Evan was stunned by this awful news.

"I'm so very sorry, my dear boy," Queen Mother said with all kinds of fake sincerity. "I'm afraid that this is the part of the story where it seems that all hope is lost. It's also the part of the story where it appears as though the hero, whom everyone has come to know and love, will lose the great battle of good versus evil."

"So there's no chance for me at all?" Evan asked.

"Nope. Sorry!" Queen Mother said, not even a little bit sorry. "You were supposed to bring me a *real* unicorn, not a silly ear of corn or some silly TV-watching Yünni

Khørn, but a *real* unicorn. And everyone knows that *real* unicorns don't—"

"*Ahem,*" King Flibbertigibbet coughed and tried to get the Queen's attention. "Um, Queen? Dear? There's something you should know—"

"Quiet!" Queen Mother hissed. "Not now. I am in the middle of some important dialogue here. I was telling young Evan here that unicorns are only a myth, which means they are not real, which also means that I win. You lose, Evan! Now you have to stay here forever and do as I say. It's all so gut-wrenching, don't you think?!"

Cynicism *oozed* through Evan's veins. "Well, *Queenie,*" Evan began, using his most cynical tone. "If you just turn your pretty little bee head to your immediate right, you can plainly see that I brought you a *real* unicorn."

"Fight it, Evan!" Bump said, rooting for his friend. "Don't be such a cynic!"

"You must resist the urge, Evan!" Ralph said, also pulling for him. "Cynical young boys turn into cynical old men! And in case you haven't heard…everyone's a cynic! Critic. Whatever."

Brrring! Brrring! "I could sure go for a hazelnut latte right about now!" Red said, trying to add a touch of humor to a very tense situation.

Evan looked like he was about to pop as he desperately fought the urge to be cynical. Fortunately, like any good old-fashioned hero, he pulled through.

"I mean..." Evan cleared his throat. "The unicorn you requested is right over there, ma'am." Evan said this very calm, very polite, and without any hint of being cynical. He nodded towards Lefticious the unicorn, who was still drinking from the water slurping thing that horses use.

Queen Mother could hardly believe her eyes. "Is that what I think it is? How lovely! I've never seen a real live unicorn before."

Everyone—including *you*, the reader—had to wait while Queen Mother gazed adoringly at the mythical creature that was no longer mythical.

(Quiet please! Queen Mother is still looking.)

(C'mon, give her a few more seconds, will ya?)

(Thank you for your patience!
Hole in the Wall continues on the next page.)

(continued)

"Well, your majesty?" Evan said when the Queen was finally done staring at the left-turn-only unicorn. "As you can plainly see, unicorns *do* exist. And I—*we*," Evan wiggled his eyebrows toward his three friends who had helped him along the way. "We brought you the unicorn. So can I go home now? Please?"

It seemed that Queen Mother didn't quite know what to say. The young boy had succeeded where others had failed.

A hush fell over the crowd. But it didn't last long. Soon all the townsfolk began to whisper amongst themselves.

"Did she hear the question?"

"Did she forget how to talk or something?"

"Does anybody have some tweezers? I accidently shoved a wad of cotton candy up my nose!?!"

"Well? I, uh...um...hmmm—" Queen Mother sputtered. "I didn't even realize *real* unicorns existed."

"Of course they exist!" Evan told her. "You just stared at it for three whole wasted pages!" Calming himself,

Evan said, "I brought it here for you, your Queenliness. So may I go home now? Please?!"

Queen Mother thought about this for a moment. She pondered the idea of letting Evan go, thereby wrapping up the story with a nice, cozy, happy ending.

Then she came to her senses.

"Absolutely not, young man," Queen Mother said. "That beautiful fairytale creature is *not* what I asked for. I specifically asked my forgetful husband to specifically tell any children who come to our world to bring me an imported Karloff Svarkskinovikosky crystal unicorn figurine. Just like the one my Great-Great-Grandmother gave to my Great-Grandmother, who gave it to my Grandmother, who accidently tried to sell it at a garage sale, but fortunately caught her mistake in time, after which it was handed down to me."

The crowd went, "Awww."

"So close!" shouted some irrelevant creature. "Shot down by a mere technicality!"

"What I did *not* want you to do," Queen Mother continued, "was to bring me the last unicorn."

"Um, wasn't that a cheesy eighties movie?" Evan asked, even though he knew for a fact that *The Last Unicorn* was indeed a cheesy eighties movie, especially since he'd seen it *fifteen* times.

"Ex-*cuse* me, little boy," Queen Mother said. "I happen to like that movie. And how does a little brat like you know about a word like 'cheesy'?"

"Are you kidding me?" Evan said, which was more snippy than cynical, so it was okay. "I learned that word *ages* ago! Every cynical know-it-all kid is a master at using the word *cheesy*. But I am no longer a cynical know-it-all kid. We've already passed the crucial hero-fights-his-own-emotions part of the story. It's over. I win. You lose."

Evan stuck his tongue out at Queen Mother.

The crowd laughed and cheered.

"That's right, everyone," Evan went on, ignoring Queen Mother and addressing the crowd. "Every main character needs to go through some kind of life-changing ordeal towards the end of a story. And that's exactly what has happened here today. I'm here to tell you that I, Evan Jacob Jacobson, am no longer a cynical little boy. I've given up the cynical life forever! Not like back in chapter twenty when I was only saying the words. This time I really mean it. It's okay, you can applaud now!"

The crowd went nuts, in a *good* way.

Then Queen Mother went nuts, in a *bad* way.

"ENOUGH!!!" Queen Mother screamed. "This trial stuff cannot go on forever. It's time for the big battle scene!"

Chapter 31
The Big Battle Scene

Suddenly, just to keep up the fantastic pace of the story, Evan, Red, Bump, and Ralph found that their hands, feet, whatever, were mysteriously un-cuffed, or untied, whichever the case may be. (*If it simply must be explained, we could just say that some nice random creature from the crowd cut them loose.*)

It was time for the big battle scene at the end!

Queen Mother stood right in the middle of Town Square, huge and terrifying, ready for the big showdown. She was way bigger than Evan and his friends, even if they climbed onto each other's shoulders, *and* stood on their tippy-toes.

Red attacked first.

Brrrring! Brrrring!

Like a fearless tricycle warrior, Red pedaled straight up to Queen Mother and began going in circles around her feet as fast as he could, which was pretty darn fast considering that some random creature from the audience (*probably the same one that cut them all loose*) handed Red a large cup of premium blend coffee. Red drank it in one huge gulp, then he went bananas.

"Take *this*!" Red shouted, going round and round. "And *that*! And how about one of *these*!" Red was pedaling himself into a frenzy, making Queen Mother really, really dizzy.

"STOP! You're making me dizzy!" the Queen shouted. "Cut that out, you hyper little boy-cycle!" The Queen's yelling only made Red go faster.

Then from the left side, Professor Ralph began to dry-heave. His whole body shook, shimmied, and shuddered in a grotesque hurling manner. It was quite disturbing to watch.

"Hey! Look at me, Queenie!" Ralph called, making sure he had the Queen Bee's full attention. "I'm going to be sick! *Hoowluh! Hoowluh! Hoowluh!!!*"

"NOOOOO!" Queen Mother screamed. "I can't stand watching other people—or dogs—getting sick! It makes *me* feel like throwing up too!"

"*Hoowluh! Hoowluh! Hoowluh!*" Ralph sputtered. It was so disgusting that even Evan had to look away. Unfortunately, Queen Mother saw him do this, then used the same look-away tactic to avoid the viewing displeasure of Professor Ralph's horrendous dry-heaves.

Then Bump moved in for the kill.

"Knock-knock," Bump said, rolling around to Queen Mother's right side.

"ARGH?!?" Queen Mother shook her bee fists in anger. "I hate knock-knock jokes! And yet I can't ever say no to them!"

"I *said* knock-knock," Bump repeated more forcefully, but still with his same old flat monotone voice.

"Who's there?!" Queen Mother asked, already starting to shake.

"Banana," Bump said.

"Banana who?" Queen Mother said, looking dreadfully scared.

"Knock-knock…"

"Who's there?"

"Banana."

"Banana *who*?!"

"Knock-knock…"

"ARGH!!! I hate this one!" Queen Mother fell to one knee. It looked like she might actually be defeated by all these severely lame tactics. "That's the worst knock-knock joke *ever!!* It's not even funny!"

Sensing that victory was near, Bump shouted one more time: "KNOCK-KNOCK!"

"W-w-who's there?"

"Orange…"

"O-o-orange who?"

"Orange you glad I didn't say banana?!!"

"Oh no!" Queen Mother had dropped to both knees. "I'm going to be defeated by some of the most ridiculous battle maneuvers ever written down! Life can be so unfair! *Aaaargh*! And why do I keep saying 'argh' like some kind of silly pirate?! *AAAARGH!!!*"

Evan stepped up to deliver the final blow.

"No! You mustn't! What are you doing to me?!" Queen Mother tried to push Evan away, but he was just so darn cute when he wasn't being a cynical know-it-all. "Don't come any closer! I hate hugs even more than being dizzy! Or seeing other people get sick! Or knock-knock jokes! Aaaaaargh!"

Evan gave Queen Mother a big, juicy, loveable hug.

"NOOOOOO!" Queen Mother wailed, finally beaten. "You've killed me! You've killed me with kindness! I'm still talking, and I'm still alive, but you've killed me, you little brat!"

Suddenly…

Out of nowhere…

For no reason at all…

Just because the Storyteller Guy said so…

Queen Mother got all her strength back. And *this* time she was even stronger than before. *This* time she was unstoppable. *This* time no dizzy spell, dry-heave, knock-knock joke, or big juicy hug could stop her.

Queen Mother went cuckoo.

BZZZZZZZZZZZZZZZZZZZZZZZZZZZZZZ
ZZZZZZZZZZZZZZZZZZZZZZZZZZZZZZZZ
ZZZZZZZZZZZZZZZZZZZZZZZZZZZZZZZZ
ZZZZZZZZZZZZZZZZZZZZZZZZZZZZZZZZ

ZZZZZZZZZZZZZZZZZZZZZZZZZZZZZZZZZZZZ
ZZZZZZZZZZZZZZZZZZZZZZZZZZZZZZZZZZZ
ZZZZZZZZZZZZZZ.

"Terrific!!" Evan yelled. "Victory was in our hands and we blew it! We blew it because of *you*, dumb Storyteller Guy! Thanks a lot!"

It was chaos!

It was disorder!

It was mayhem!

It was y-tiliu-q-nart!

It was the exact opposite of tranquility!

The ground shook. Buildings crumbled. Everything was falling to pieces. The wacky world of *Hole in the Wall* was about to be destroyed. Queen Mother was going to smush everything. She was going to punish everyone just to show the readers that sometimes life isn't fair. All the creatures, the sweet innocent townsfolk, *everyone* began to get vaporized by Queen Mother's secret weapon: her stinger.

"HELP!!!" one helpless creature shouted. "Queen Mother is stinging all of us helpless creatures with her gigantic stinger and vaporizing us!"

"Yeah!" hollered another helpless creature. "And if she continues on her path of destruction, then none of us will make it back for the sequel!"

"Ahhhhh!" some nameless creature screamed.

"Help me!" screamed another.

"I'M SCREAMING!!" screamed a third. "CAN'T YOU TELL!?!"

Queen Mother kept flying through the air, stinging everyone in sight, going completely insane. All the while, she laughed her maniacal, sinister, evil laugh. Laughing and stinging is all she did. Queen Mother kept stinging, and stinging, and stinging...

And stinging...

And stinging...

And stinging...

And stinging...

(For the rest of the page!)

And stinging…

And stinging…

And stinging…

And stinging…

And stinging…

And stinging…

And stinging…

And stinging…

(And most of the next page too!)

Then Evan woke up…screaming.

Chapter 32
Just a Stupid Dream? What a Rip!

Yep! Just like all of those cheesy cop-out endings, it was all just a *dream*. After all the wild, crazy, weird stuff that happened, Evan woke up to his father shaking him.

"EVAAAN!" father said. "Wake up!"

"Whuh? What happened?" Evan slowly opened his eyes and found himself lying on the floor of the basement with a huge goose egg on his forehead. At first, he wasn't sure where he was. All sorts of strange visions were bouncing around inside his head.

Two seconds ago, Queen Mother was destroying the Town, the Castle, the townsfolk, and his friends with her huge stinger. And now, he was in the basement, lying on the floor with a throbbing headache.

"Oh, look at that huge bump on your head," Father said as he checked out Evan's swollen noggin. "That's one giant goose egg you've got there, son. What happened? Did you hit your head on the table?"

"I...I guess so..." Evan let his father help him to his feet. "I'm not really sure what happened? I came down here to get some glue so I could fix Mom's broken unicorn figurine. And then I—"

"Mother's unicorn figurine?" Father's face turned pale. "What happened to it? You didn't break it, did you?"

The crystal unicorn was in Evan's hand.

Inexplicably, it was back in one piece.

Evan couldn't believe it. He just stood there staring at the 100% *un*broken unicorn figurine in his hand, wondering if *all* of it had been a dream? Beginning with him breaking the crystal unicorn in the first place.

"How did—? When did—?" Evan was relieved, but also very confused. He felt kind of re-con-li-fuse-ved, a combination of both.

"Evan?" Father said, with his arms crossed. "Why do you have your mother's favorite crystal unicorn figurine in your hand? You know you're not supposed to touch it."

Evan placed the figurine into his father's outstretched hand.

"That's better. Now, let's get you upstairs and put a Band-Aid on your boo-boo. But first things first, let's put your mother's very expensive crystal unicorn back in the glass display case, okay?"

"Yeah, okay," Evan said, being led back up the basement stairs. He didn't have to bother checking over his shoulder for basement monsters since they never attack kids who are with adults. "But, um, Dad?

"Yes, Evan?"

"Can you please not call it a boo-boo?" Evan said. "That's baby talk."

His father looked sort of upset, or perhaps a little sad. He'd always talked to Evan like this. Now, at this very second, Evan's dad was having one of those moments that fathers have when they realize their little boy is growing up. In just a few short years, Evan had gone from cutesy wootsy baby talk, to real talk, to cynical brat talk, to please-don't-talk-to-me-like-I'm-a-baby talk. And even though none of the life-changing experiences that Evan just went through had been fully explained to him (*whether they were real or imaginary*), Evan's father realized that his son was a changed man. Boy. Whatever.

"Okay, Evan," Father said, nodding proudly to his son during this nice cozy ending. "I can see that you've had some kind of out of this world experience that has deeply affected your outlook on life. I promise, from here on out no more baby talk."

"Thanks, Dad."

"Now, let's put your mother's unicorn figurine back in the display case before she gets home. Otherwise we'll *both* be in big trouble. Deal?"

"Deal," Evan said. Then they shook hands like adults sometimes do. "Hey, Dad?"

"Yes, Evan?"

"How about after I finish my chores, we go out for coffee?"

"Coffee? I don't think your mother would approve," Father told him. "But...okay. How about decaf?"

"Okay," Evan said.

"Besides, there's something else we need to talk about," Father said. "Your mother and I…um…"

Evan knew what was coming next.

Father said, "Well, let's just say that you might be getting a little sister at some point during the next few months."

Evan said, "Yeah. I know…"

Wasn't that a nice happy ending?

But the story doesn't end there…

Chapter 33
One Week Later

A lot happened during the week after Evan had his otherworldly experience, which he *thought* really happened, but probably didn't, but *might* have really happened due to some bizarre plot twist that might suddenly pop out at the very end.

On Sunday, after drinking a delicious cup of sugared-up coffee with his father in the kitchen—which he had to promise not to tell Mother about, even though it was decaf—Evan hopped on his bike and rode down to The Hub, a local convenience store within acceptable traveling distance for a young child.

Once there, instead of buying a bunch of candy for himself to pig out on like he usually did, Evan spent his entire allowance on a big scrumptious chocolate bar. Instead of eating it, he raced home and put it in the fridge with a note that read:

For my class, Dad.
DO NOT EAT!!!

On the following Monday, before class started, Evan marched right up to Mrs. Towne's desk and told her the truth. He told her the whole story, beginning with how he'd seen the Spelling Bee words written on the page, how he went home and looked them up in his father's dictionary, wrote them on his hand…

Everything.

At first, Mrs. Towne was really mad. But seeing how hard it was for Evan to tell her the truth, she couldn't help but feel at least a little bit sorry for him. So sorry, in fact, that she marched Evan up to the front of the class so he could apologize to everyone else.

And even though it was a very, *very* hard thing to do, and even though it made him very, *very* uncomfortable,

Evan went through with it. He stood there in front of the whole class, looking guilty and embarrassed, with his face all red and everything, and told them that he was really, really, *truly* sorry. He stood up there and took it like a man. Adult. Whatever.

At first, everyone was really mad. But seeing how hard it was for Evan to stand up there and make a fool of himself, explain what he'd done, apologize to everyone, *and* ask for their forgiveness…

His classmates couldn't help but feel at least a little bit sorry for him.

Then a weird thing happened.

They forgave him.

"That's okay, Evan!" Shelly McCrombie said.

"All is forgiven, dude!" Dustin Baker said.

"Yeah, don't worry about it, man!" Eric Dooley hollered from the back of class. "I cheated too!" Actually, Eric shouldn't have admitted this because he also got into trouble.

Afterwards, Evan felt good about telling the truth. However, since he *did* cheat, Mrs. Towne still had to punish him—and Eric Dooley, too. Their punishment was that they both had to sit out during the next *two* Spelling Bees. It wasn't so bad. The two of them sat at the back of the class and cheered everyone else on.

It was fun.

Better yet, Evan made a friend.

Chapter 34
One Week Later-er

Kids at school weren't sure what drastic change had come over Evan. All they knew was that he was different somehow. Evan walked kind of different, and kids noticed. Evan talked kind of different, and kids noticed. Mainly they noticed that Evan wasn't such a rude, obnoxious, cynical kid anymore.

The world was a different place now that Evan Jacob Jacobson was no longer a cynical, know-it-all kid. He was content just being a *regular* know-it-all kid.

When it came time to do his chores the following Saturday, he went down into the basement to get the glue a second time. Not because *he'd* broken anything, but because his father broke something—a *lamp* if you insist on being nosy. This time he wasn't the least bit scared of running into the silly old Washing Machine Monster.

But this time, between the freezer and the junk shelf, right next to the very same hole that was usually covered, the steel grate had conveniently fallen off. There was a hand-printed sign right next to it.

Evan leaned in close to get a better look.

The sign read:

FREE rice cakes!

Then a big, green, scaly hand reached out...

And grabbed him.

YAY!!!
The *real* end.

Thank you for purchasing and reading *Hole in the Wall*.

Handersen Publishing LLC is an independent publishing house dedicated to creating quality young adult, middle grade, and picture books.

We hope you enjoyed this book and will consider leaving a review on Goodreads or Amazon. A small review can make a big difference.

Thank you.

Tevin Hansen is the author of numerous books and short stories. He currently resides in Lincoln, Nebraska, where he enjoys writing and illustrating books, skateboarding, reading half a dozen books simultaneously, and chasing his two small children around the house while singing horrendous versions of children's songs.

Find out more at: www.tevinhansen.com

Shaun Cochran has illustrated a series of books produced by the Sanford Harmony Program of ASU and has several more books on the way. He is very interested in comics and graphic novels, having exhibited some of his work at the Arizona Comic Con and other pop-culture venues. You can discover more at ShaunyRedComet on RedBubble and Facebook.

More books from
Handersen Publishing, LLC

Also from Handersen Publishing

Stinkwaves started in 2013 as a zine, but has now grown into a "mega-zine" filled with the works of talented indie authors, poets & illustrators from around the globe. Each issue is packed with short stories, flash fiction, poetry, illustrations, and author interviews.

Discover more at:
www.stinkwavesmagazine.com

Handersen Publishing
Great books for young readers
www.handersenpublishing.com

CPSIA information can be obtained
at www.ICGtesting.com
Printed in the USA
BVHW080149250419
546397BV00005B/44/P